BLOOD RELATIONS

BLOOD RELATIONS

A NOVEL BY
CARLOS MONTEMAYOR

INTRODUCTION BY
CARLOS FUENTES

TRANSLATED BY
DALE CARTER
AND
ALFONSO GONZÁLEZ

Plover Press
Kaneohe, Hawaii
1995

Printed and Bound in the United States of America

Library of Congress Cataloging-in-Publication Data

Montemayor, Carlos, 1947–
[Mal de piedra. English]
Blood relations / by Carlos Montemayor ; introduction by Carlos Fuentes ;
translated by Dale Carter and Alfonso González.
p.   cm. — (Plover contemporary Latin-American classics in
English translation series)
ISBN 0-917635-16-7 : $17.95
I. Carter, Dale. II. González, Alfonso, 1938– III. Title. IV. Series.
PQ7298.23.0688M313   1995
863—dc20   95-1265
                                                              CIP

Acknowledgements
The translators wish to express their thanks to the author and to Catherine
Rendón Cavanaugh for their valuable assistance and suggestions.

Distributed by Academy Chicago Publishers
363 West Erie Street
Chicago, IL 60610

Introduction

This is a rarity: a social and political novel with philosophic depth and poetic height. The immediacy of the social situation—work, poverty, the mine—becomes even more immediate when it suddenly ceases to be experience and becomes destiny. This happens when illness, fatal illness, and then death, fatal death?, become the real reality of poverty, work, the mine. I put a question mark next to the fatality of death. Why? Because if the fatal illness does lead to death, death, truly, has preceded the illness. Montemayor is a Mexican writer. He knows the secret of Mexico, which is that death precedes life, that we all descend from death, that death is a part of the embracing whole of life. Death had to be in order for *us* to be. Montemayor, who is also a classical scholar, brings a Latin precision and clarity to his tale of work, death and relations between fathers and sons. Without the pathetism of a D. H. Lawrence, this is more like Virgil entering yet another dark pit of hell. His Mexican Dante is also immersed—this is important for the reading of the novel—in the world of religion, but the Mexican Catholicism which permeates the book is a syncretic affair, much too tainted by ancient Indian beliefs to be totally "Western." So there is also a blood tie to an ancient Mexican past, a tie to the land and those buried in it before any European set foot in these mountains and began exploiting the dark silver womb of Mexico. A profound sense of humanity, of shared suffering, of the will to be, pitted against the fatality of survival, permeates this moving novel by Carlos Montemayor. Realism in *Blood Relations* is really real, not an ersatz documentary. Its reality is its language, its poetic pain and beauty.

Carlos Fuentes

For my son Emilio

My Brother
1
(May 4, 1955)

"Everything's included in the service," he tells me. "Coffin, candles, pedestal, candlesticks, and hearse. Look, come this way. This one doesn't have a double lid, but it'll keep the body in good condition, better than a wooden one. It's upholstered, of course, and the lining is all one piece . . ." I look down at the floor, at the tiles on the floor. I keep my head down. I have to go over to the mine to get paid. I can't afford something like this. Then there's Helena and Antonio's kids. All of them in two rooms. And the constant struggle for money. "Here are our wooden coffins," he tells me, "the Curtained Model or the one with the Sorrowful Mother . . . Right, this is the Sorrowful Mother, covered with cloth . . . It has sawdust padding under the lining . . . Or maybe you prefer that one over there; it's just plain wood painted black. It's called The Bandolón." I'm hungry. I can't bring myself to look him in the eye. Fuck it! It's always the money. You need money for everything . . . I need a beer, or a mezcal. That's right, a beer and a mezcal. But that's what pisses me off, the fact that he's my brother, precisely because he's my brother. ". . . look at the Curtained Model . . . It would be just like this one, except that the size would be different since it's for an adult. Yes, just like this one . . ." I look at the coffin he points out. It's a small coffin for children. The cloth cover is already yellow. It's ripped in one corner. I look at the ribbons hanging at the sides. I lift the lid and see the tacks and a tear at the base. Yes, Antonio, this is where you're going to be, in this, in this. I hear the noise he makes behind me as he searches for some papers. I notice that I'm thinking about nothing, that my mind's a blank, that my head is beginning to feel hot again. I need money this week. I'll go up to the mine to try to get my pay, to see if they want to pay us. It's different when someone is no longer here, that's all, just not here any more, Antonio. I feel hungry again; I should have eaten something before coming over here. But with Antonio there . . . No, the children shouldn't be there. Although my father used to say that it was all the same, that it didn't matter whether you saw this as a child or as an old man . . . I have to get paid; money overdue is a double debt. I see the walls lined with coffins. My mouth feels dry. I ought to go find Gregorio, or any of the others. I'll look in at the "Four Roses." Or in the pool hall, right, I'll look there too. Beside the desk there are several candle holders with red cylinders. I'm getting embarrassed; I can feel it in my face. As if Antonio were someone else, not my brother, not the one who died this morning, but something else. "The color changes according to who it's for," he tells me. "For an adult, it's black. The ones for children are always white . . . There's no sawdust under the lining, instead it's newspaper cut into strips . . . We'll do all the rest, that's right . . . We'll take everything you need for the wake right away and tomorrow we'll come by at whatever time you say . . ." He's my brother, yes, my brother. Forgive me, Antonio, but I'm really broke. I can't do anything else right now. Times are bad for everyone, for you as well as for us. My eyes are burning. I feel something like an explosion of salt in my eyes, and my throat is burning too. Fuck it! How it hurts to lose a brother. I'm sleepy. I have to wait, to wait.

"Excuse me, sir, yes, thank you, thank you, excuse me."

My Brother
2

I feel the blow from the heat as I go out into the street. There are lots of people around; the sun is heavy, hot. My eyes are burning. It's from lack of sleep; I need to rest and eat something. I should have accepted the job on the semi; it was the best thing to do. I shouldn't even have thought about that job at the mine. I only did it because Alfredo insisted. Everything he has anything to do with turns out badly. It's better for me to go with Pérez today; he can try me out. Gregorio ought to be here by now. I can smell the enclosed, sour odor. Francisco is in the bar. He waves to me. I make my way between the tables. There's Gregorio. I feel sad. I don't know what starts this sadness. I become aware of the heat, my thirst, the smoke, and the voices from the tables. The photos of nude women cut from calendars are still hanging above the jukebox; I can also see the calendar with a picture of a river and two boys fishing. Gregorio has spotted me; he's with Manuel's brother and Alfredo Montenegro. He's always smiling like that, huge, fat. I go up to Gregorio. He's sweating. He slaps me hard on the back so it hurts. I sit down at the table with them. Suddenly it seems to me that there are lots of people in the bar. Chepo sets a beer down in front of me and returns to the bar. Alfredo asks for another one for himself. They're already drunk, and they slur their words as they talk. Alfredo's face is red. Gregorio is sweating. It'll be a long time before they put out the snacks. The beer is cold and I feel the bitterness in my mouth.

"Have you got any trips planned?" I ask him. "I need to go on one tomorrow, Gregorio . . . Or maybe you, Alfredo . . . Is there any work on one of Robles's trucks?"

"I have a trip for the Vásquez family," says Gregorio. "You can come with me, but we have to leave tomorrow."

I drink my beer. I take a little salt. I'm really hungry. I'll eat something on the road after I leave.

"I'll go see Pérez," I tell them. "Maybe he'll take me on as the driver of one of his semis. I can at least try. I'll tell him I was a friend of Hector's, that we were going to work together."

"That guy from the Ahumada?" Alfredo asks. "He's got very little work. He doesn't pay well, and these days he only makes trips within the state . . ."

"I was planning to go over to your house tonight," Gregorio tells me. "But if you need something, I can come sooner."

"That's okay, tonight'll be fine, Gregorio." I see the dirty wood of the table, the glasses, the cigarette butts. I hear the music that's beginning to play and I'm aware of the voices at the other tables. "What about those guys from the Ocampo mine? Did they pay you, Gregorio? Did they pay you everything they owed you? We should stop them from contracting for more trips until they pay us. They owe me for two months' work. Let's go together, Gregorio, and stay there until they pay us."

Alfredo laughs. Then he shouts at Chepo, reminding

5

him that he hasn't brought him his beer. He picks up the cigarettes from the table and offers them to us. Manuel's brother gives me a light. We all light up. I didn't ask him about Manuel, that's true. He's in Santa Bárbara, down in the mines just like everybody else. Alfredo offers to buy me another beer. It'll soon be noon. There are lots of people. Gregorio is sweating. He looks at me. He takes some money from his pocket and offers me a hundred-peso bill.

"Payment in advance for the trip," I tell him as I put the money away. "Take it out of my pay for the trip, Gregorio. Deduct it right now."

I'll look for Pérez. My mind's a blank, but I'm still sad. I feel an urge to get away, to find work, to sleep all after-noon. I tell them that we're burying Antonio tomorrow at ten. I feel the heat. The beer is ice cold. It's better for me to get up from the table. I want to get paid today. Alfredo starts talking about Durango again, about the Ro-bles mine. I look only at his thick, white hands. I still feel like I'm in a hurry, Antonio, an urge to get away, just like when the day is over and you keep on working. I'll go to Triplay again; it's good to insist. I'll check the trucking lines in Santa Bárbara, too. Maybe they're adding more trucks. I hope so; maybe that way I can manage even though the work is exhausting. But I still feel rushed, An-tonio, because losing a brother is always painful, even though there are more immediate things to think about, or causes for regret. Lately I've recalled what we did, what we saw as children, what you used to say about the mines, about Villa Escobedo, about women; to remember is to hear all of it again. Also the envy I felt because you were going away to Villa Escobedo, or because you already had a woman while I had to jerk off thinking about what you used to tell me and desiring Ofelia, whom I saw every morning across from our house as she raised her skirts to wash the floor. But I felt envious as a brother, Antonio, not as a man. It was envy and pride at the same time because you already had a woman, already knew how to have her. And when we went up in the hills together I saw what you did, how you cut the rattles off the rattle-snakes, and how we would laugh when the rabbits would leap up like white, spongy stones breathing rapidly. But it was just that they were running, and there was no way that we were going to catch them. Those days I thought a lot about Grandfather Refugio, about his death, about when I used to go every day to the cemetery when I was a kid. The same drought, the same poverty, the same problem with the heat, the fatigue, the lack of sleep. Antonio, when I found you drunk, I wanted to hit you for getting that way, because I was sorry for not having done it before, because it irked me to know that it was okay for you to do what you had done; and you got scared without knowing what I was saying to you, without even hearing me, with a blank smile on your face caused by the mezcal and the lack of sleep. Antonio, my brother, those few days when I brought you the mezcal and watched you get drunk, take the bottle, look at the sky without seeing it. Another urgency was added to the rest, a sense that the days had not passed, that we were here before all this, before the heat, before the storms, before the blood that stained you and left you with those sad eyes, like a woman's or an animal's, that made me talk continuously about silly things, of memories that are no longer mine. It's the urgency, brother, the urgency of being a brother, the urgency of having to know each other here, in this life, of having to attach ourselves to it only to have it jerked away.

Extreme Unction

1

By means of this holy unction and His most pious mercy, may the Lord forgive you all that you have sinned with your eyes, the life that entered your eyes to the point of separating you from Him, the arid plains that caused you to curse heaven, which is the work of God, and the land which is the work of His hands. God forgive you because with your own eyes you saw the days, the time that God gave you to live, and your wife and your children and the ground where you made love and slept. God forgive you for the stinking carbide that guided you deep within the ground, without seeing, to excavate the mine tunnels and for closing your eyes when you were inside your wife, or any woman when you felt that life was building up within your body and was powerfully gushing forth and making your breath short, and you closed your eyes because your life was exploding inside that woman, because your accumulated life was going to pieces just like your conscience, and your dreams were all that remained to anoint your poverty and your old age and your eyes and never another regret except for living here, or for the mine, or for the blood, or for the corrosive blindness where you found a tiny loaf of bread and there was only room to bite God's repentance, knowing that you sinned against God because He is the merciful one and the eyes that search Him out see Him when they are humble, although they are as blind, as hungry, as abandoned and as sick as yours.

My Grandfather
1
(July 10, 1931)

I go out to the corral and hide. The wall is hot. I see the loose, dry earth and lie down on it. I open my eyes with my head resting in the dust. The stones seem very tall; I try to pick one up. I'm hungry. I'm also sleepy. I brush the dirt from my head and face. I imagine that it's night-time and that there are many trees and bushes and that nothing can be known in this darkness; I'm in the middle of it and I shout out loud, scream, but without speaking, without anyone's hearing me. Then I open my eyes ever so slightly and look at the sun, the hot afternoon, and I rub them, and the sun burns me, and I think that I'm keeping watch over the afternoon like God and that no one can come in here, in my forest, except for my grandfather Refugio, so that he can be with me and come to the corral with me. I get up. I'd like to go down to the railroad station and stay there. Or travel, see all the hills, so as not to go to sleep. Like my brother Antonio. He's working in Villa Escobedo now. He refused to stay here. If he were with me I could tell him that I feel something else now, not just sadness, but something else. But it's not necessary. Now it seems to me that he's someone else, not just my brother, but someone else. Like Manuel, for example, but Manuel is not my brother. My eyes burn. I shut my eyes tight until they hurt. Now I open them and everything is far away; the afternoon is very big, but it's far away. I go into my house. My sister Julia sees me. I sit down beside her on the earthen floor. The aroma of the flowers is quite penetrating, as if it were another person amidst the heat and the voices; and his body smelled like that, of flowers. They're going to pray for my grandfather again. I lie down on the blankets that cover the floor and feel a prickling in my legs. My eyes are still burning. I feel like crying again. I don't want to get up. My grandfather is here, stuffed into that long wooden box. I cry, I bury myself in the covers, but I cry anyway. My head feels hot, as if I could hear a lot of children laughing, like lighting several bonfires in the hills, because it was always going to be night, so that the noise from the creeks on rainy nights could be heard, a noise like the clatter of stones, the sound of banging on trees, of knocking walnuts to the ground at night.

My Grandfather: Refugio's Dream

2

With its trees all clumped together, the grove sinks into the fog. We are passing close to the trees, but at times we lose sight of them. The noise of the cart can be heard on the road, among the rocks. The mules shake their heads; their hooves rise and fall rapidly and with great force. The driver raises his head and looks at the white clouds that advance across the sky, keeping pace with us. I see the trees nearby, right beside me. I stand up and reach out my arms to touch the green and white leaves on a cottonwood tree; they seem like crystals of glass, or water. I can't seem to touch them; the cart trembles but doesn't advance. I pull in my arms and sit down again; I look at the grove in the distance on the floor of the valley, enveloped in fog. The driver is a stranger, but he's my friend. He shouts at the mules, and I sense the presence of his smile there under his hat. The cart rocks back and forth, but we still don't move. The mules stand motionless. The earth is slightly dark and so is the sky, as if it were dirty. I feel like running now, turning around to look at the cart stopped in the middle of the road, far away now, with the driver sitting there looking at me and smiling. There are many dead bodies on the ground; they're scattered all through the hills, lying face down. As I run, I jump over them or dodge between. Someone grabs me by the arm. It's the driver; he holds me still with one hand and with the other offers me bread. I eat and start to run again. I realize that the bodies are weightless; they seem empty. I begin to turn them over, but they are all faceless; they have a dark stain that first appears to palpitate and then is still. They're all hollow. I notice a fresh, clean smell. It's getting dark very quickly now. The cart is becoming lost in the darkness. I run toward it, and with a leap clamber up to where I was before. I hear the soft noise as the mules piss on the ground. They finish pissing and we start to move forward again. The driver says that we've crossed the grove several times. The shadow cast by his hat has disappeared, but I still can't see his face. The sky is clear. For a few moments now the road has become broader, as if the horizon itself were becoming the road or it no longer existed. I am carrying walnut leaves; they seem to grow bigger, and in the branches small green spheres appear like juicy marbles. I cut off a couple and throw them to the rear of the cart; they stain the wood with a dirty, mossy green that starts to melt into droplets as if it were sweat. The driver laughs; I look at his eyes and nose, his mustache and beard. I'm looking at my Grandfather Refugio. He smiles at me. I tell him that I thought he was dead. I'm sorry for having said it, but he seems not to have heard. I look at his bony hands, his long hard nails, his fingers grasping the reins. I look at his large, wrinkled head. I can just see him turning into the street on the opposite side of the road, moving through the crowd. The crowd pulls me to the other side. I shout as loudly as I can. I still feel happy for having come along with him.

The house is dark and very big. The walls rise very high;

I can't make out the roof. Many men and women are talking and drinking. I look at a boy running through the orchard, carrying the branches and dry leaves that are falling from the trees. There's a man among the walnut trees, beating on the branches with a long staff; he's been beating them, but no nuts are falling; just the sound of the blows can be heard. I'm hidden behind a chair. Someone takes me by the shoulder, and I'm frightened to see the boy smiling right beside me; he invites me to come along with him. Now we gather up the branches and dry leaves and lay them next to the orchard fence. The man has ceased striking the trees; he observes me fixedly from above. We begin to throw rocks at him and numerous blackbirds and wild pigeons take flight, and birds that I'd never seen before begin to fall. I run toward the birds, but as I touch them they disintegrate like clods of earth or dry leaves. Many more birds of the same kind fall to the ground; we lift our heads and they fall on us like so many whispers of cloth and we place them near the fence. I hear laughter. There's a three-year-old child on the fence looking toward the river. I climb up on the fence and look across the river. Several women dressed in black come down the hill accompanied by some old women and walk over the stones, picking up something that I can't make out. I see the dry river bed covered with stones. Yes, over there is my house, behind those corrals. The women are talking among themselves, but from time to time they turn to look at me and wave their arms. The boy climbs down off the fence without my noticing and begins to play in the orchard with the other one. I want to climb down, too, but I can't. Something prevents me from jumping. I yell at them, but they can't hear me. I move near one of the trees; I try to get down by hanging onto the trunk. The boys are stand-ing in front of me, making fun of my efforts. They throw rocks at me. In the distance I seem to see Grandfather Refugio with several men. With a leap I drop to the ground. I begin to feel afraid of being with those boys. I run to the plaza. The people stop me from going any far-ther. I take a detour through a solitary street only to run up against the crowd again. The two boys point at me; they're standing among several women. It's easier to look for the cart and then for Grandfather Refugio. I reach a group of people having a meeting. When I ask them for my grandfather, they take me by the hand and we go into a very large room with green walls and many chairs. They say they were waiting for him, but that he has not re-turned. I'm frightened. I don't want my grandfather to die again. I leave that place and run for a long time. I scream and scream again, crying with all my might.

My Grandfather
3

I become aware of the earth's smell. My eyes still burn. I rub them, but they burn all the more. I've cried while I was sleeping. I see my grandfather's coffin and the lighted candles. It's nighttime now. Someone is next to my sister Julia. I observe her; it's a woman I don't know and she's asleep. There are still people here. I look at the door that opens onto the corral, as if the darkness were standing there looking inside. My body feels as if it's gone to sleep and my head is hot. I remain here, sitting on the covers, doing nothing. I lean my head against the wall. They've placed the table next to the door; several of the chairs don't belong to us. People are talking quietly as if I were sick with a fever and they're talking low so that I would get better, so that I'd feel well. In the other corner my mother is with two women. I hear a noise in my ears, like a whistle that doesn't stop. I feel as if I weren't awake yet. I look at the door once again where the darkness waits like a familiar animal. It's hot, but I'm cold. My mouth is dry. I feel as if I were missing an arm or a shoulder or something. Julia comes over to me. Her hands are hot. I look at the ceiling, the beams, the walls of the room.

"It's a long time until dawn. Keep on sleeping. Go on," Julia tells me. I don't answer her. Once again I hear the whistle of the silence. The women speak louder. "I'll give you something to eat before we start to say the rosary," she says.

I get up. I go and stand near the table. She gives me a cup of hot coffee and some bread. Her eyes are red. I feel a desire to caress them, to put my hands on them. The women who were out in the corral come inside. I like to eat my bread by itself, without anything to drink; I feel it in my mouth as if I had been eating it for a long time. I look at the long, black coffin that contains Grandfather Refugio; I look at it for a long time without thinking of other things. I squeeze the bread in my hand. The coffin is surrounded by lighted candles; I smell the aroma of the flowers. The women and some men with their hats in their hands begin to kneel around the coffin. I see all the women with rosaries in their hands. Doña Soledad begins to pray. I close my eyes; I know that she's speaking; I know her voice as if I had dreamed it many times. The other voices begin, but all together they are almost violent like a dry creek on a rainy night that runs only when it rains, just as hollow trees fill with water only in the rain. I squeeze the piece of bread; I like to feel it in my hands. I want to take a few steps, touch the coffin for a moment, go over to Doña Soledad and be with her. I want to cry again, but my eyes hurt even more. My father realizes that I'm watching. Doña Soledad is speaking again. They listen to her, paying careful attention to her prayers. My father is looking at me, and one of my sisters is, too. The prayers of everybody together make it seem as if many people lived here and we didn't need to be afraid because the house is full. I bite into the bread; I take two bites, enjoying the flavor. I finish eating it. They keep on praying. I need to piss. I go out into the corral and feel cold. Suddenly, it seems to me that I can hear the silence again, just for an instant. I feel the earth under my feet. There are many stars. They palpitate like wounds, as if all of them were talking or falling little by little, coming together to stay here in the corral forever. I piss in the corner where we have bottles and papers piled up; they sound hollow, empty. I no longer feel cold; actually it's hot. I cross the corral and try to open the wire gate that has gotten stuck. When I open it, the hens near the fence become frightened. The kids from the house next door are watching me through the window. At Manuel's house the light is out and the door is closed. From here I can see my house where all the people dressed in black are kneeling around Grandfather Refugio's coffin. My name is the same as my grandfather's. When I was born, they wanted me to have the same name as my grandfather: Refugio. I sit down in the dirt. God sees everyone there in the room where we live, just as I see them from this place where I'm seated. I hear the murmur of many angels who come down from the stars to sit beside me in the corral and watch the people praying. We're sitting here waiting for them to continue. It seems to me that the angels will go inside from one moment to the next, as if the people inside were bad and are doing nothing only because Doña Soledad knows very well what steps to take. I lift my head and look up to the sky: God's face can be seen, stained with stars, covered with a mist like clouds that come out of every star at the same time and cover Him. But God is opening His eyes behind all those stars. He sees me and sees the patio full of angels, all sitting on the ground, and He sees the room where my grandfather is and looks closer in order to see my grandfather better and hear Doña Soledad, and I feel that in my house my grandfather is all alone, and that the women surrounding him are really dark angels, but God has seen them and will know what to do. I close my eyes, searching for the voices, and seated here on the ground I can listen to them. I hear the silence once again. If Antonio were here, too, I could hear even more. I remember him, walking with me inside the station, talking to me about Villa Escobedo. I can also see him cutting mesquite pods at the foot of the hill. I'd like to talk to Antonio, who never should have gone away. But my father said yes, that it was okay.

"It's okay, yes, it's okay for you to keep on working. Because there's almost no work for miners anymore. If you've got a job, it's a good idea for you to go even though you aren't old enough."

"You don't understand," Antonio told me later.

But Dad said that right now all the miners are fucked and you have to work whenever you can. Dad can only work two days because all the miners here in Parral are in the same boat, although they let some of them work three days a week.

From the corral I can see the hill that marks the mine over there. I can't hear anything. At times, yes, I can hear the sound of the mills. Antonio told me that I don't understand. He said it when I went with him to the station. I went along with him carrying his carbide lamp. He told me that the lamp was all fucked up because it had belonged to my grandfather, but that he was still going to use it a while longer. At that moment I recall the odor of carbide; it's a very strong smell, as if coming from something alive and hot.

Extreme Unction

2

*By means of this holy unction and His most pious mercy, may
the Lord forgive you all that you have sinned with your ears, the
names of the things with which you came into this life and led
you away from Him: the heated noises of the night and the mines
that filled your ears with dust when in the inmost depths of yourself you waited for the detonation of the charges of dynamite, the
blows of the pick and the jackhammer as though you were some
other body, some other saliva—these heated noises that were not
from God but covered you so that you couldn't hear, you who
did not hear God, who were born in despite of God and lived
and sinned in order to hang onto life and succumbed to the deafening voice of things; may God forgive you because you only
repented*

> *of the world in order to sink even deeper in it, to give it more
> children, to hear everything, the noise of the trees, of the leaves,
> of the women,
> of the children, of the men, of the drunkards, of the whores,
> of the rivers, of the rain,
> but not to listen to God who mercifully would have guarded*

*you if you had listened to Him before you were born, and upon
being born, and after being born, so that you would not have
known this world, neither its joys nor its malice nor its nostalgia;
and that is why your prayers fell like stars from heaven and were*

cast in the open wound of hope that never heals, but rather becomes deeper, and you were left with a hunger to hear, because you heard only your own voice, and your punishment was not only to remain with the hunger that your parents and your wife and your children knew, but with a hunger to hear more, to hear life and not to satiate yourself with God's life, because now the silence of death has no limits nor hours nor fatigue; now that no one is hurting you, understand once and for all that only His voice can bring peace to all those ears which are tormented by life.

My Grandfather
4

Very few people remain. My father stands smoking next to the door. There's a strong odor from the cigarettes and the flowers. I'm hungry. I'm going to sit by my mother and sisters. My brother Antonio said that my grandfather would not die this week but next, and that he would be back on time. He told me this when I went with him to the railroad station. He was very quiet and I could look at him without his noticing. I don't believe that he was thinking about my grandfather anymore. He said that there was a lot to be done, that in Villa Escobedo one has to be tough, because everyone is like that. I didn't answer. We went up the street to go around the station. We saw the railroad cars scattered along on the rails and off in the distance the water tanks. Everything smelled the same: the railroad ties, the pumps, the offices. A few new ties were piled up next to the water pump. Several men were crossing the tracks carrying tools.

"It won't happen this week, but next," Antonio told me. "I'll make it back in time."

We waited outside the offices. The warm air smelled like oil, like the railroad; that's how the whole station smells. From the platforms we could see the town: all the houses stuck to the hills, to the earth. Behind us the hill where the mine was looked like something live. Many people were walking next to the mills on the stairs at the miners' entrance.

"Villa Escobedo is not that important," I told him. "You can wait a while longer."

He laughed as he turned to look at me.

"You can't possibly know," he told me.

I didn't answer, even though I knew it wasn't right. Nor did I look at him. He tried to look into my eyes. But my father had said yes, for him to leave.

"They fired all the miners," Antonio told me. "You don't understand. Villa Escobedo is going to disappear. Almost everyone has left . . . There's no work, see? That's why I'm leaving, because I have a job. Later I'll go to San Francisco del Oro because they're hiring miners there. You don't see anyone on the streets; it's very lonesome, completely fucked up."

But I wanted to get to know Villa Escobedo. Grandfather Refugio told me many times that Villa Escobedo is better than our own town. He was already twenty-eight when he came down from the mountains to work in the mines, but that was his business, even though it fucked him all up, as he used to say. The river is nearby and there are trees. But I didn't say anything to Antonio. If he were here now, sitting next to my sisters, or seated over there, next to the coffin with Grandfather Refugio inside, with all the smell from the flowers, then I would tell him that I dreamed about Villa Escobedo a while back. But that I dreamed it was different. That I went with Grandfather and there was a fiesta in the town and we got lost there. But I would have to tell him that I don't want to be here, but with him. He is my brother; that's why when he finally understood, he would say:

"Yes, next week we'll go together."

When Antonio got on the train, he said goodby with a smile. He didn't say anything else about Grandfather Refugio; that's how I know he wasn't thinking about him, that he didn't have a reason for leaving. I stayed on the platform until the last whistle died out, and then I sat on a bench as if I were waiting for the next train to leave. It was very hot. There weren't any people around. From where I was I could make out all the houses down below among the hills, and here I was at the station surrounded by quietness. I could hear a few shouts from men who were crossing the yard, or who were repairing engines or tracks, but they seemed to be in another town, and I imagined that I was someone else and that they knew me. I waved at them, but they didn't see me. I thought that this was the way that the railroad station at Villa Escobedo would be and that after resting a bit more I would walk down with Antonio and I would tell him that we were going to work together. I left the station, but I stopped to look at it many times. They were beginning to move some freight cars to another track to form lines for loading freight. I walked down by the power station. It was already very hot. But I began to feel this strangeness that is still with me, this annoyance with Antonio. I'm the only one who has been here, and not him, and he doesn't think about this. He's my brother, but as a brother I feel pain for his actions; it is as if I were doing them myself. That's why I get angry with myself, because partly I must be like he is.

My father comes into the house now. He stops for a while. He looks at me. He asks me what I'm doing here.

"I was thinking about things," I tell him. I look at his hands. They are dirty, stained, like Grandfather's. His fingernails are broken, split. He's wearing the same boots that he wears to work. I'm barefoot. I look at my feet; I haven't washed them since this morning.

"I slept in the afternoon," I tell him. "I'm going to be here until it gets light."

He remains silent, not answering. He looks at my mother who's sitting with the other women. Since Grandfather's illness my father hardly speaks. Every afternoon he would sit next to him though they hardly spoke to each other. He had free time because they didn't give my father a steady job at the mine. They didn't fire him, but they only hired him on Thursdays and Fridays. And he can't go anywhere else; he said there was nothing he could do. That's why he spent the afternoons smoking, looking at the hill, like Grandfather, but without saying a word. He would only pay attention when Grandfather started to hemorrhage and his beard and clothes would get all bloody. My grandfather would curse when they cleaned him or when the hemorrhaging wouldn't stop, and Dad would say yes, but without really meaning it, only so that Grandfather wouldn't be the only one saying something. Then Grandfather Refugio would close his eyes and his breathing would become more difficult; he would make a sound like that produced by words, but very soft or very deep. But they weren't prayers, they were names of things, or memories of things, or curses, but he would recite them in order to have something to do, quietly, because he didn't need to speak to my father. I used to sit with them, but my father wouldn't notice. All at once he didn't realize that we were there, and he wouldn't even hear me. My grandfather would look at me for long periods, and sometimes he would talk to me. He had a hoarse voice that I liked, very deep, like that of a strong old man. At times Antonio and I would bring mesquite pods so that we could eat with him. Grandfather would take the pods in his enormous, bony hands, and it seemed as if a monster held the small husk and then crushed it. Breathing with difficulty, he would open his mouth to chew, and then his lips, his beard, came apart; it seemed like a great effort, as if great power were needed to separate his lips and beard so that his heavy breath would come out, and the pods surely felt that the world was devouring them because of the great effort he was making, the great power that my grandfather had. My father would remain with us, looking at us; sometimes he would take a mesquite pod, but only to hold it or play with it, not to eat it. He would bite on the husk a bit and then spit it out into the street. My grandfather spoke in a low, thick voice, and he would get angry because of the heat, because it wasn't raining, or because the blood stained his clothes. This happened to him once when Antonio and I were with him. Grandfather was listening to us and suddenly he opened his eyes sadly, called himself a son-of-a-bitch, and said that he was getting a fucking nosebleed; and from his nose came the dark blood advancing steadily like an animal. Grandfather breathed with difficulty through his mouth as he tried at the same time to spit out the blood. My father cleaned him up and called my mother, who then took over. My grandfather either closed his eyes or looked blankly at my mother, who was cleaning him up and dampening his beard and forehead. My grandfather's eyes were wet, opaque crystals. That time Antonio didn't do anything; he remained seated looking at Grandfather and almost immediately got up. Later I went to find him and we walked around the hill.

"It was an ugly sight," he told me, without looking at me. "It nauseates me. It's silicosis . . . I see it in Dad," he said.

I had thought about this before But for me it wasn't nausea, it was fear, and I could see it in Grandfather as if a hill, or many hills, were gushing forth water or blooming with the sound of life, but not nausea. Grandfather seemed stronger, and I was scared only when he spit out the blood that always filled his mouth and then continued spitting because he had the taste of blood in his mouth and was trying to get rid of it. Antonio didn't understand.

"All miners die like this," Antonio said on another occasion. "They end their lives all fucked up. All of them . . . The same thing happens in Villa Escobedo. Grandfather is still alive because he began working in the mines late. He was twenty-eight. But he won't make it past fifty-two; he's already too sick. That's why he was one of the first ones to be fired in Villa Escobedo; there were a lot of miners in Veta Grande just like him, and they were all fired. Not like Dad; he was younger when he started working in the mine, like me, at fourteen. He, too, is all fucked up. You'll soon see what I mean."

And it hurt me to hear it from Antonio because a brother's actions are always painful. But I didn't tell him, I only let it show when we were hunting for pigeons; I made an effort to be a better pigeon hunter than he was just to prove to him that I didn't need his advice, that I could do this by myself. Because Grandfather had taught me how to hunt and how to look for squirrels and how to set the traps. And Antonio also knew, but he had learned on his own, and not like me who had learned from Grandfather Refugio. Antonio laughed that time. And it got dark early, or rather without our realizing it, and in the darkness it seemed as if neither one of us had a face, or that each of us had a different face even though we were still the same, and then I had the courage to tell him that what he'd said wasn't right. He tried to look at me and told me that I couldn't understand. But I had trapped more pigeons than he had, and without his help. Then he laughed, but he didn't mention anything about the pigeons I'd caught without his help, and he began talking about Villa Escobedo. Yes, I still don't know what Villa Escobedo looks like, but I feel that I already know it from what I've heard and that I will see the fields and before getting there I will say:

"Yes, that's the one."

Antonio also changed, drawing away from Grandfather, because before he wanted to be with him and they used to go together to Villa Escobedo. One day, I walked with them part of the way; it was the first time that I saw the station. The noise coming from the locomotive and from the men who were repairing the rails and the ties and who were helping to hitch the railroad cars; all of these sensations were like a part of me. I liked it very much. I didn't want to leave that smell behind because everything, the water tanks, the railroad cars, and the benches on which people wait outside, all were one smell. That's why I didn't realize that they were leaving together even though I also wanted to leave, not to go with them, but so I could ride on the train. But Antonio began withdrawing from us, and when Grandfather became ill he didn't want to be with him anymore. Not even when my father also started to change. It was when they shut down Veta Grande, when they fired Grandfather and when they gave my father fewer working days. Even though they pay him less, Antonio's still at the mine; at least he has a job. That's why he's there, because he has a job. I also have a job, but in Rodrigo's store, where I work with Manuel. Mother is coming toward us. Now she stops next to my father. She tells him that there's a bit of rice left, for him to sit down and eat.

"I'll fix some camomile tea, if you want," she tells him again.

My father doesn't answer; then he looks at me. I smile, but it's not easy, because it's difficult for me to smile, too. Not for Julia, it's easy for her; she knows how to smile when she wants to. I see my father in front of me, tired, eating at the table without looking at me. I stay there, close to him, to keep him company. My mother sits with us.

"I'm going to stay awake till dawn," I tell my father. "I already slept in the afternoon."

He gets up from the table to go to sleep and walks toward his bedding, which is on the other side of Grandfather Refugio's coffin. Mother is now clearing the table. Suddenly I feel alone, as if I had had many things which don't exist anymore, as if I had had a life, a house, and now these were all gone. I'm afraid. The night weighs heavily as if it were alive, as if it were a body or a place. Some of the women linger; they don't say much. My mother sits with them and looks at me. If Antonio hadn't left, if he were here, we could talk and I would tell him:

"Have you ever felt like I do? I can't trust anything anymore. I'm afraid of something. I don't know what it is."

The lighted candles are next to the black coffin, which is covered with flowers; it smells like flowers or dry wood.

Blood Relations

I can see the nearly frozen flickers of the candles. It is as if night had stopped in order always to stay here, to remain here tonight, so that nothing else happens. The room seems very silent, though I can hear the voices of my mother and the other women; in the coffin there is complete silence, as if the candles and the coffin were deep in thought and I could hear them, as if God and his angels were watching over my shoulder, waiting for night to pass, waiting for dawn like me, surrounded by this silence, as if all of us were standing around the coffin, allowing Grandfather to rest.

My Brother
3

And what did Antonio have to do with all of this? What did my sitting next to him for hours at a time, useless like him, smoking the whole afternoon, hearing only his silence, ignoring him, growing tired of his illness, have to do with this? It wasn't my brother, it was a senseless thing next to me like the heat or the cigarette, or the hill, and only his hemorrhaging would bring me back to him; his agony and his waiting for death nauseated me. It's true. He is my brother and a brother always has the power to wound. My wife, María, didn't change. It's the truth, while I turned into someone who didn't know how to speak like a man, a brother, who couldn't explain what didn't interest him, those things that were Antonio's when they were still recognizable. But suddenly I would realize that I was with him. Not that he was next to me, but that I was there in the same place as he was. I didn't know how to tell him that I had discarded all that from my memory and couldn't remember that we were there. And that's when being with him would make me furious, when it was unbearable to be beside him and absorb his illness, his uselessness. I couldn't bear to feel tied down to him, to the brother who used to take me to the whorehouse and pay my way and hand me over to the whore, not allowing me to join in the conversation and the insults. Because by taking his younger brother to a whorehouse so he'd be scared, and then not letting him sit at the same table with him, was to Antonio something like further proof of his manhood. Why did you do this to me, Antonio, even though you loved me, even though I was your brother? But in spite of this I loved you, Antonio, I loved you. Later I found out who you really were. I had already been in Talamantes for several years far away from your house, your wife, your children. You'd forgotten me while you went down into the mine and I became more of a man and still didn't feel the need for children, not until I went back to Parral. This is because they shut down the textile factory in Talamantes. And when they did, they shut down the town. Then I found out what it was like to be buried in this town and get all fucked up deep inside, just like everything in this country gets fucked up, just the way it happened to you and Grandfather in Villa Escobedo. I returned to Parral, and I didn't want to have to take orders from you again, working myself to a frazzle like you, until I found employment with the Chávez brothers, with Alfredo Montenegro. I ate a different bread than you, the same, but different. But everything we lived, everything that happened between us each day, divided us because there were many things, and when there are too many things, too many days, these weigh heavily and you can't move freely because the load is overwhelming and pulls you apart. During the afternoons you thought more than I did, and I drew away from you, Brother, remembering what had always united us. But you didn't talk in order not to interrupt us; even though neither one of us could ration the days with the measurement of light or of hope. You, Brother, with hope for life because you always waited for the last day after tomorrow, and I with hope for a life that shits on me this morning, all alone.

Extreme Unction
3

By means of this holy unction and His most pious mercy, may the Lord forgive you all that you have sinned with your sense of smell, the life that led you to the odor of this world but not to the fragrance of God, the world that entered through your nostrils with all its life, like the spirit that gave you life, all the way inside you, so that you could know Him in that innermost place, in your soul, where the bloom of your life could be found and where there was no room for God because you chose the scent of a woman and of the world, but not God's forgiveness, even though it would have cleansed you of the stench of poverty and of life so that you would come purified to Him, you who always came home to the smell of the chairs, of the blankets, of your woman, of the walls; and when you smelled it you knew it was your home, that it was your true home where you could later prove it to yourself with each child, with each embrace of your woman, with each dream in which the blankets remained on the dirt floor with the smell of your food that could never satiate you, the table at which the smell of the mine never left you, the carbide lamp that got up when you did, the mine like a blow from hard, dry earth that hurts, that wounds, that seems to love but that wears out your breathing and undermines the body; and you never had a word of forgiveness for God; you preferred to feel drunkenness inundating your shallow breathing when the metallic-tasting blood gushed from your *nose, as if another mine inside of you wanted to surface and achieve cleanliness or forgiveness without repenting for having been away from God and being close to yourself. Instead you despised His scent, even though God's aroma is His spirit, the breath of life, because this is what His breath is like, because that's what His smell is like, because that's the way it was going to be for you while you were dying in the mine. God, like air, is never ending.*

My Grandfather
5
(July 11, 1931)

I wake up and the light hurts my eyes. Julia tells me to get up. My father is already up, and I hear him talking in the corral. I smell the dirt floor where I sleep. I get up and see the black coffin where Grandfather Refugio is lying.

My mother is talking with my sisters near the table. I go out to the corral. The sky is very clear; it's going to get warm very soon. I can feel the dirt under my bare feet. Manuel walks up to me smiling, but he doesn't talk to me; he only looks at me. I take some water from the bucket. I set the washbasin on top of a rock. I don't close my eyes and the water covers my hair, my forehead, and I stay like this for a long while. Then I straighten up and close my eyes. I feel as if the rain were falling, drenching me, and I feel that I am somewhere else, that I'm someone else. I wash my arms and the water drips down my shoulders and back. I stay like this waiting to get dry as I walk in the corral. Manuel follows me, smiling but without speaking. I tell him to wait for me, that I'll be back soon. Now I go into the house. I put on my white shirt and comb my hair. My sister Julia tells me that I didn't wash my feet, and for me to go do it.

"In a little while," I tell her. "As soon as I comb my hair."

I'm hot and hungry. No, it's as if I were incomplete once again. Julia is already dressed in black, just like my

mother. They tell me to come and eat breakfast because
it's already served. People begin arriving at the house. I sit
next to my father; I kiss his hand and then pick up a tortilla.
From here I can see the coffin where Grandfather lies. I
sip my coffee and then start eating my beans. I squeeze the
tortilla tightly without anyone's noticing it. My father is
just finishing his meal; he's talking with Rodrigo, the
owner of the store. They laugh. My father is finished and
he gets up from the table. Julia is behind, leaning on my
chair. They talk loudly, not like yesterday evening when
they spoke more softly. I feel that people are very far away
as if they were scattered out. I try to eat a bit more, but I
can't finish. I remember Antonio at the railroad station.
He told me that I didn't understand. He's told me this
several times, whenever I tell him what I feel, what I don't
agree with. I don't finish my food, I just drink my coffee.
I'm nervous, as if I were waiting for something to happen.
I walk close to Grandfather Refugio's coffin. I go out to
the corral; Manuel approaches me.

"About ready?" he asks, smiling.

"No, not yet," I tell him. "But it's almost time."

I fill the washbasin with water and begin to wash my
feet. The water is very cool. I look at Manuel who is sitting
on the ground, next to me. I think he already washed his
feet, but they're dirty again because he's walked a lot
around the corral. I carefully dry my feet. Manuel looks at
me as I pick up the washbasin from the ground. I dump
the water next to the wall.

"We're going to leave in a minute," I tell him. "Wait
for me. I want to go outside."

"I'll go with you," Manuel tells me.

"No," I tell him. "I want to go by myself."

I go out of the corral. In the street there are several grackles that fly over the houses. The street is dusty, already hot. I sit under this tree as if I were waiting for Antonio to appear at the end of the street, dressed in mourning. I begin to climb the hill. It's already very hot. There are many rocks on the hill and it feels very hot. I look at the mesquites near the river, and then at the cottonwoods and walnuts in the fenced orchard on the other side. I look way over there, close to the bridge. It's hot. I'm nervous. I can see my house from here along with the adobe walls of the corral. Now I know that Antonio will not come today. I begin to climb down from the hill.

I go into the corral. Manuel is down at the end, at the front door of his house. I go into my house and I see many women sitting down and many men standing around smoking and speaking softly. Among the flowers I see the big black coffin where Grandfather Refugio is lying. I'm scared; I feel like crying. I want to see Grandfather Refugio, but I don't want to cry. I feel a sharp pain as if I had been running very fast and suddenly had crashed into an unseen wall.

I go across the room. People are blurred in my vision. I sit without saying a word, feeling that I am about to cry, that I'm very sad about the whole thing. My father puts his hand on my shoulder and leaves it there. I try not to move so that he won't take his hand away. The candles surrounding Grandfather Refugio's coffin have stopped burning. Now they are very small; they burned out during the night, while I was asleep. With the break of day a lot of things take shape, and many people, although it's still hard to see. I feel crowded as if everything is in my way. My sister Lourdes cries again; she covers her nose and eyes with a handkerchief. She's sitting next to my sister Julia. I know that she's clenching her teeth in order not to scream. I don't feel like crying anymore. I don't feel anything inside me; no, that's not true. It's as if something surrounds me that is not there. I think about Antonio, that's all I think about, that he's far away, and I don't feel anything else, not even anger; I feel only that he's far away, that he's not here. My father takes his hand away from my shoulder. Someone gives him a cigarette and he lights it. He smokes. Rodrigo is talking to him. The cigarette turns to ash very quickly and falls to the ground at his feet. I'm very hot, but I'm also quite calm. My father gets up and leaves. I hear him asking a question outside. Manuel is looking at me from the door. My father returns with several men. I know them. They say it's time for us to leave. They remove the flowers carefully and set them on the ground near the corner where my sisters are sitting. They take the candles out to the corral to throw them away. My father walks over to the coffin and closes the lid. Then, between them, they pick it up. My sister Lourdes starts to cry again, but this time she really screams because now they're really going to bury Grandfather Refugio. The men set the coffin on their shoulders carefully to make sure that it's secure. Balancing the coffin on their shoulders, they leave the room, holding their hats in one hand. The coffin sways slowly as if it were alive, breathing, as if it realized it was being taken away and wanted to wake up. Julia is also crying, without screaming, but she's crying; I can see her beside Lourdes. But as the black coffin passes through the door, I hear voices of women and men, speaking softly and momentarily remaining silent. I'm looking at the effort of these men as they walk. Everyone is standing and looking at the coffin. I feel that everything is rising, that a sea of black rises up around me. Many black bodies stand up, and I know that this is what God would feel, that I'm seeing myself as God does, and I don't know if He's looking at Antonio too. And angels hide in the rising darkness, and only God remains behind. He doesn't follow me. He doesn't go out with us.

The coffin goes out through the street door to encounter the hot sun. I hear everyone's footsteps. And now God is among all those black bodies who are filing out into the sunlight. And the same hot dust that burns my bare feet hurts Him as well. And no one sees Him. And the light hurts my eyes. As it reflects off the ground, I feel my eyes burning terribly. We all walk along behind the coffin where Grandfather Refugio lies without speaking, without spitting on the ground, not cursing the heat, but feeling the sun, the hot morning inside the coffin. God comes among us and I close my burning eyes so as not to step on Him, so I won't notice if I step on Him because if I do, I'll be lost forever; and I close my eyes so I won't see. But I sense everyone's dragging feet, the loud sound we make as we walk along. We're walking down the street now. From here I can see the dry river bed, the white stones that cover it. Manuel catches up and walks along beside me. And I feel that I am about to vomit all the peace I had inside. But it's as if everyone had left me all alone. And I feel God inside me, just Him, hurting me because He's walking through the hot dust burning his feet. But He's everywhere and nothing happens to Him. And I have to scream, I have to cry, I have to open my mouth and shout because God is with me and He is stripping me of everything He gave me, everything I had inside of me, and it hurts, but He can't know that I have to cry, but I want to cry, and I can't hear Him because I want to cry.

Extreme Unction

4

By means of this holy unction and His most pious mercy, may the Lord forgive you all that you have sinned through your taste, all the bread, all the meat, all the food that never lost its savor in order to satiate you, the names of all things which drew you away from Him; and they learned the taste of your voice, the dirty name of hunger, the virile curse that makes every word a living thing, the mine in which you saw your sweaty and dirty body and your hands stiffened by the bloody steel pick, just so you can now feel your saliva, your mouth, doubting whether time really passes by, whether outside of the mine in the town the afternoon still contained light; you were vaguely remembering something which at that precise moment you were forgetting forever, and you felt the word spurting from your mouth, from inside you, and it felt like a piece of salty bread that quenched your thirst, but that you spit out immediately like water from a bitter spring, a curse on everything you were thinking, a remorsefulness, a memory that is regret, that is the silence beneath the deep voice, a voice that was lost because of your not having chosen God, and that is why the voice fell from above like a morning star and it was the true voice, dangerous, the one that causes sin or accepts it, and also the one that redeems; and through it you repented of having lived with hunger, with foremen, in so many mines and through so many days which left the taste of silver in your mouth, with the blood that flowed from your nose leaving its taste in your mouth like a new sin or a new word that ignited and suffocated your life, a voice difficult to understand; and God remained far from you because His voice was not like yours, because He is merciful and takes pity on the men with no voice; and His voice sounds like the wind, like the remembrance of the rain; and whoever heard it will never be thirsty again, nor hungry, because in God there is only one word that created you and formed the world; that is why His voice returns to Him when you die without having heard Him, because He was always next to you, near you, waiting, because on account of the word of God you were given life and nothing can take away your death, because one word of God is many places, many lives, and your life will be indistinguishable from His voice and you will never again know it.

My Brother
4

I'll have to come back later, maybe even tomorrow. To-night's better. But I have to sit up all night with Antonio. No, I can't do it today. When I get back from that trip with Gregorio, I'll look for him. I'll wait for him until I get to see him. But I need that job; I need to talk with him. My head is very hot. But I also want to collect my money. I need to get some sleep; I can no longer stand this heat. But I need sleep more than anything. I can think later. Yes, later.

"Yes, I know the gentleman when I see him, but I'll look for him later . . . It's a job-related matter, ma'am. I'll come back later, thank you."

She closes the door. I have to sleep a bit. I can't stand the sun. And this hunger's killing me. But I can't just think about that and nothing else, no. I need to think about something else. There is a lot of dirt around here; every-thing is dusty. Tomorrow I'll be able to make that trip with Gregorio. Antonio used to do the same thing. He left so that he wouldn't have to be with my parents and my grandfather. He told me that I couldn't understand. But I don't understand even now. Yes, we had to change. When he came home already sick, we knew he had come to die; we didn't say it, but we already knew it. And then we realized that we had been separated for a long time.

Because someone doesn't just die all of a sudden, no. Antonio knew it; he said as much to me one day several weeks after my father had died. He came home drunk. He shouted at me from the door. I felt relieved to be with Antonio, but it was uncomfortable for him. I had stayed home because he wanted to leave, to ignore my sisters and my father, to live in peace. That was after I returned from Talamantes. Even though at that time we were already separated by having lived differently and by the very memory of having done so. I was working in Talamantes when I began to show signs of reaching the limit of what makes men strong or different, that makes us individuals. Antonio said goodbye the night before I left for Talamantes; he stayed for only a moment; he had a drink without saying much. I felt that he had understood me and that was good, for I was leaving the house because I was a man, not because we were brothers, and understanding me was a sign that we were brothers even though Antonio perhaps didn't understand my embracing him, and he repeated "good luck." In Talamantes people were different, more open, less harsh. And I don't know if Antonio realized it, if he knew that I sought other places in order not to run into him, because it's all right for brothers to run into each other, but not for men to. When I returned to Parral, I came back home because the textile factory in Talamantes went broke and Antonio was about to leave. My arrival helped him because the lack of work made me stay home. And with me there, he could ignore everything, leave when my father's silicosis was already quite advanced. And this was something else that separated us, because he realized what was going on. I understood it in part because we were brothers, and because since Grandfather Refugio's death I had realized what Antonio was like. When I returned we didn't talk to each other the same way because each one of us already had his own interests in life, and we drew apart even more when he left the house. We were already men; we got together a few times to drink, and when we went to the whorehouses I couldn't have the same woman that he had just had because we were no longer just brothers, and sharing prostitutes among men is something else. He gave us money, yes. He provided money for the house, what little a mine worker gets. But his soul, his spirit, was defective. Either he was stronger than I was, or he knew more. I don't know. But my father said that it was okay, that it was okay even if I didn't understand it. But Antonio knew more about me than he did about anyone else in the family. He would say that it was I who should stay. That I should stay because I wasn't a miner like they were, because I was the only one in the house who didn't work in the mines. And that's the reason why, when my father died, when three weeks after we buried him, Antonio came to the house drunk and shouted my name from the gate, but wouldn't come in. We went out together, but I felt no happiness, only the desire to cry. Maybe this was the love one feels for a brother. Above all we were brothers and we talked a bit, but each word was like many words compressed into one, and in order to talk we got drunk. A brother's actions are always painful because it's as if you were talking to yourself; because partially you're alike, the same things happen to you. Suddenly Antonio looked down as if he had remembered every day that we had lived together, everything that we had thought together, so that I would understand, as if once again we were walking toward the train station a few days before my grandfather's death, as if my father's death brought everything back to him because one death brings back memories of other deaths, not sorrowfully, it just stirs them up as if they were being arranged in our memory, as if memories were being shuffled around so as to make room for the new death which was finding its place in our memory until we also die; then all of us can be reunited again.

"So that you'll understand," he told me, "I don't know how to say it . . . Death is something that belongs to you, not to anyone else, it's yours. Because it's not just a matter of someone's dying and that's all there is to it, but you have to get involved, you have to help him do it right."

My God, it took me a while to understand it, not because I didn't feel it, but because one doesn't know how to decide to think or to continue to live. Antonio's memory is painful to me now because it's as if it were myself, because I have to accept that he can't continue to live in me after he has died. And a brother's actions are always painful. Antonio, I have to walk beneath this sun. I have to think about working, about what they owe me, about the semi I want to get in order to have a steady job, about your wife, your children, about the changes in your household, about the sun, about the hunger I feel while I try to forget about you and that when I'm free everything will have already happened so that I won't feel how you're dying inside me, but that I'll find you already lost within me and I won't bother you, and you won't stun me like the sun, like the regret at having been brothers and my remaining here now and your retreating to Villa Escobedo to avoid Grandfather Refugio's death and in Durango running away from my mother, but now at least you won't be getting drunk as you did at my father's wake.

Extreme Unction
5

By this holy unction and His most holy mercy, may the Lord forgive you all your sins of touch, because your hands touched the world like a blind man trying to hang onto things, everything from people to your own life, from your bed to the food that you felt in your hands before eating it as if your hands ate first, as if receiving charity would allow them to know the bread or the food before putting it in your mouth, already half-eaten and inadequate. May God forgive you for the sin that made you wear out your hands by holding objects, for every time you held onto something, it would wear out your life, your heart, because you would take the whole world in your hands, all the objects in the street, in the mine, in your house, the faces of your children whom you caressed, the dust during times of drought, the metal that did not surprise you any longer when it was separated from the veins in the rock and which you contemplated like a drink of black water, brilliant or reddened, poor as a counterfeit coin. May God forgive you because you touched a woman, because you touched her body, her waist, her thighs, her breasts, her moans, as if it were the only gift that men condemned to poverty and forgetfulness could afford; and may He also forgive you because He allowed you to know that you were dying when the blood began to flow from your body as if it wanted to leave you before you died, and you felt your life, your own breathing locked up inside you, imprisoned by your

*body as the mine seized you, as the landslide caught your com-
panions and your hands could not go into your body to save you,
to dig, and you did not look for God, you did not think about
your repentance even though you were created by God's hands,
from the hands of His mercy and His well-being, even though
His hands also dug a cavity inside of you, a place for your soul,
something untouchable from where you never were able to escape,
or from where you emerged as if from Paradise never to enter again
and to remain in the world, in the harshness of things, in your
own hands that never formed a breath nor a life as God did with
you. Through forgiveness His hands made you new in order that
you could discover God's touch deep inside of you, His merciful
touch that gave you life and which you took from His hands, only
to remain eternally without it.*

My Grandfather
6

Now we all kneel once again, and the altar boys ring the bells. One of my father's friends is beside me, his hat between his legs, his hands immobile. Manuel sat further back. Now I see him; he is disheveled and sweaty. Julia didn't want to come, she stayed home getting everything ready. Father said it was best that way. He told me to come alone, and I thought that Antonio should also be here. I've been thinking about this for quite a while now. But I don't want to think about it because today I shouldn't think about it. "You can't understand," Antonio told me, and after he left he never once thought about Grandfather again. Now he is in Villa Escobedo and he probably can't imagine that I'm here, in church, attending mass, thinking that what he did isn't right. My father spoke with him, but Antonio said that he would be back in time. "I'll be back in three days," he said. I'll wait for him down at the station tomorrow to see if he really is coming back. Sometimes Antonio and my father talk, but I'm not allowed to be present. Once Antonio told him that both of us couldn't do it. Later I asked him what he was talking about, and he told me that it wasn't any of my business, to stop pestering him. I didn't insist because Antonio is moody, and sometimes he takes me downtown with him,

or down to the train station, or hunting squirrels or pigeons. The priest just said my grandfather's name again:
Refugio. I turn around so I can see Manuel. He's looking
at me. The priest blesses everyone with the sign of the
cross. Grandfather Refugio didn't like to pray, he said,
because it was a lot of work and nobody had ever taught
him how. He would hear my mother and my sisters pray.
He looked at them gravely, quietly, and when they were
through he would continue doing whatever he was doing
before. He would be the same person again. I know a
prayer and part of another one. I've been saying them ever
since we arrived at church so that I can help too. I've been
saying them even though Rubén says they're a pack of
lies, but he's a Protestant and is going straight to hell. He
says that it is written in the Bible that there is another
death, but that there is no eternal hell, a hell that forever
torments those who deserve it. I told him to come see the
priest; he didn't want to, because he said that they don't
study the Bible here and that neither the saints nor the
priests nor hell will fool him. But that's because he is a
Protestant; that's why he says such things.

Once I dreamed that I was here alone at night. I told
Grandfather, but he didn't pay attention to me. I dreamed
that I was near the altar, and as I turned around I saw that
the church was closed. It was very quiet but I could hear
a sound as if someone were breathing inside the church
and watching me. Then I felt a little scared, but not overly.
And I looked at all the statues to see if one of them was
making the breathing sound, but it wasn't any of them. I
walked up and down the aisles and it seemed to me that
many of the statues hadn't been there before. I came upon
a new room full of statues covered with white and purple

shrouds, and I said to myself that I hadn't seen this room before. Then toward the end of the columns I noticed a statue covered with a dark cloak, and I thought it was breathing and alive and this scared me. Its bare feet protruded from beneath the shroud, and it was standing on a globe covered with clouds, and I noticed that one foot was moving. Fear overcame me and I ran toward the door. But when I got there, everything was very quiet and it was very cold, and behind the wooden door I seemed to hear many whispering voices. I lay on the floor so that I could see underneath the door and I saw a long plain, a very long plain. The sun was shining and next to the door I saw the feet of many men and women walking back and forth, waiting to come in. I stayed in that position for a long time because I liked the sight of the plain. A boy was looking at me with pitch black eyes and a disdainful grin; his face was familiar, but I couldn't remember him. He seemed to be talking a lot under the door, laughing, but I couldn't hear him. Then I saw his lips pronouncing my name. He said that this was his name and for me to move because they were going to hurt me. I got up quickly and I managed to see that someone was behind me, and my legs began to hurt and I wanted to cry, but the barefooted man was seated on the bench next to me. Then the doors opened and the people began to come in from the plain, brushing up against me as they went by. It was like a fiesta because there were shouts and laughter and people were selling things. Then the man pulled out a dark cloak and covered me with it. I felt the cloak over my head, on my face, and could feel my breath in the dark. Then I saw myself up in the air and knew that I would begin to fall forever, that I wouldn't be able to save myself, that I wouldn't ever meet anyone else. I felt very sad and started to cry. Then I woke up and I told Antonio that I was afraid, but Antonio was still asleep and I don't know what he answered. I kept trying to wake him until he told me in a clear voice to go back to sleep, that it was still very early. Then I went outside and sat against the door of the house in the night. I felt all right, but only for a while because later I felt like going in again. It was cold; the night was silent and the moon lit up the whole street, the whole hill, the whole sky.

My father and the other men get up to carry the coffin outside. Mass is over. The man next to me also gets up to help them. Once again I can see how the coffin seems to be alive as they move it to place it on their shoulders and then take a step back. Manuel signals to me: "It's going to fall." I check to make sure as the coffin moves past us. My father is at the head of the procession. I can tell that he's deep in thought and doesn't notice me. Now Manuel and I follow along behind. I feel the coldness of the floor as I walk. Everyone makes the sign of the cross as we go by; people follow behind us, and I can hear the footsteps again. I can see the sunlight in the street; it's very strong. I see people walking in the plaza. Manuel doesn't say a word; he looks very serious. There are very few of us; we occupied only a handful of benches. The coffin is passing through the church door now; I feel the heat and the light hurts my eyes. The coffin moves now as if the pallbearers' eyes had also been hurt by the sunlight. Manuel closes his eyes and shields them with his hand. As we move down the street I begin hearing the sound of the steps, of the dragging feet, the noise that all of us are making. I want to tell Manuel what I think about the noise. I would certainly tell Antonio. The coffin receives the full blast of the sunlight.

"Grandpa would be swearing like a mule driver."

Manuel looks at me again. "They're going to hear you," he tells me.

I feel the warm earth beneath my feet. People on the street stop to look at us and everyone takes his hat off. I feel their eyes on the coffin, on us, Manuel and me, and I try not to look back at them. I try to walk along watching only how the coffin sways. I hear the footsteps. I feel that God has returned to earth again. Manuel makes an effort to look serious. I don't remember how Grandfather Refugio used to talk before, how he happens to be in that box, feeling the heat of the sun, of the morning.

Because Manuel and I have been working together in the store since last winter, we talk a bit. I tell him about Antonio and what he tells me about Villa Escobedo, about his work, and about all the miners who have been laid off and about their empty houses. We are planning to go over to Villa Escobedo and unexpectedly drop in on Antonio. Someday we'll just go to the station and get on a train since we already have the money. I won't tell Antonio so that he'll be surprised when he sees us, nor Manuel so that he will be surprised when I say:

"Yes, this is it. I know the way."

I remember what Grandfather used to say, which way you have to go, where you have to cross the creek. Last winter we spent a lot of time with Grandfather. After work at the store we would cover up with his blanket and listen to him till late at night. One time Grandfather went outside with us. The entire world was cold; the sky was overcast so that you couldn't even see the clouds. The wind was very cold. And Grandfather told us to touch the earth, anywhere, and when we touched it, it felt warm, very warm, on the hill, on the street, beside the other houses. He told us that the earth was always like this, that it was never cold, except after a storm, and then it felt cold. That's right, in the afternoon when we finished at the store we would buy cookies and candy and then go home. We would sit next to the corral, where dry tree trunks lay as if asleep in the cold. When we walked at night Manuel's nose got even redder than mine; our noses would begin to run, and we had to wipe them continuously. We would go running home and seek refuge beneath Grandfather's blanket, where we could feel his enormous shoes. We would offer him cookies because he didn't like candy.

In the winter I wore shoes. Antonio brought them to me because it was cold. But we would listen to Grandfather talk about the town, about Villa Escobedo, and he would recite one *corrido* after another, and I liked to hear him sing because he never did, and his voice would be hoarser, but I liked to hear it come out through his stained beard with much effort, as if the voice were very old, very rusty, very hoarse. He told us about all the deaths that had happened in Parral, the ones he had witnessed, how they would talk before they started killing each other, or how the problem had developed to the point that they would threaten to kill one another the next time they met. He used to talk a lot about Nicandro and how they used to sing together accompanied by his guitar. How he just happened to be there and joined in the hunt for the killer of Augusto's nephew. How he went to talk to Villa because Villa was going to execute his father-in-law and how Grandfather went to beg him not to do it, and Villa received him just for a moment and said, yes, of course they we're going to hand the man over to them right away, right after they shot him. Then my grandfather explained to Villa what his father-in-law had done when the Gringos arrived, that he had collected that money so that they wouldn't kill any more people, that he wasn't going to keep it for himself. Villa called one of his men and told him to free the old man that they were going to shoot at noon and said that he didn't want to see him again, that he didn't want to be bothered with him anymore. Grandfather saw him the next day when he was riding across the Guanajuato bridge, and Villa smiled at him. After that he ran into him several times in the vicinity of La Villa de Grado, but Villa didn't recognize him anymore even though Grandfather continued to greet him. When Villa was shot, he went to look at the car, but he couldn't see it because there were a lot of people and Guillermo Baca Street was under guard. Manuel and I have been to the corner where Villa was riddled with bullets, and we've seen the tree his car crashed into. We spent that entire winter with Grandfather, but Antonio would always go out and didn't spend any time with us. Grandfather said that that was how it was with men, that it was a good sign. That's why Manuel cried when Grandfather Refugio died, because he had learned to love him. And I told him that we felt like brothers because we had both been with him and had been working together. Then there was the time when he went out with us. We walked the uplands for a while, and he had us throw rocks far away because rocks bothered him. Everything looked dry, and the land seemed to be without protection. Not like today, even though it's also dry and covered with thicket and underbrush. But the heat changes the land considerably; the strong sun loosens and warms it. During the winter the sky looks as if it had been sifted or rather unsifted because the cold stays up there, and it drips down slowly, making everything slow, making us feel far away when we look at it. Once it snowed, but just a little. Grandfather said it wasn't going to rain this year, that when it snows a lot, it rains a lot during the year, and that when only little icicles form on the eaves, that when the frost kills everything, there won't be any rain, and that's what happened. That time we went up the hill only a little way so that we could see the town from above, with its white river meandering everywhere, and the bridges all over town. Manuel got sick because he'd gotten up during the night and he didn't put anything on. And I went to visit him at his house because he didn't go out that afternoon. I was able to stay with him until dark since in the afternoon there was very little snow left, only slush. When I started home I couldn't move my mouth; I could hardly speak, as if my jaw were in the grasp of many hands so that I couldn't move it; that's how I felt on account of the cold. Last year I really enjoyed winter; who would have thought that it could change so much?

Now we are in the main square, skirting the market and heading toward the last bridge. Manuel is very tired; he is also sweating and he doesn't look at people anymore. His mind's on something else. I hear the footsteps again. I don't feel that God is on Earth anymore, I feel something else. Sometimes I don't hear anything except that I feel the sun above me. It's very hot now. One can't think straight, and everything seems to take longer. I see Grand-father's coffin swinging back and forth and receiving all the heat, the full force of the sun; it must be very hot. If someone were to touch it, he'd burn himself. The men are tired, weighed down by the coffin they're carrying; their shirts are drenched with sweat, and they're holding their hats in one hand. Their steps are heavy and they drag their feet in the dust, raising clouds that seem to give off more heat. We are now on the bridge; it's the highest one and you can see how the riverbed winds its way out of town through the hills. Manuel looks at the dry riverbed; along its banks the houses are made of planks and cardboard.

I don't need Antonio. I am growing used to the idea that I don't need him. He didn't want to be here. He knew what was going to happen and he chose to leave. But it's not necessary for him to be here. It's not necessary. I don't know how to say it, but we don't need to be with him. I have thought about it these last few nights and also when Manuel and I were with Grandfather last winter. The only difference is that before I used to be sad when I thought about it because he's my brother, and a brother's actions are always painful. But these last few days I'm not sad anymore. There is only one more street to go and then we'll arrive at the cemetery. But it's still a long way. I hear our footsteps as if someone were beating the ground to the rhythm of our dragging feet. It is as if someone were dragging something from inside us. It's as if a hot rain wanted to erupt from the ground.

"Manuel," I say to him. He comes over and looks at me.

"Close your eyes and listen to the sound we make as we walk. It seems like rain."

He closes his eyes, manages a broad grin, and then opens them again.

"Yes," he tells me, but I was already thinking about something else.

He laughs and closes his eyes again, but then opens them and doesn't say anything else to me, but smiles once more as he wipes the sweat from his face. Two of the pallbearers tire of carrying the coffin with my grandfather inside. We stop; dust rises around everyone who has stopped. I feel my feet burning. Manuel tugs on my arm.

"He's going to fall," he tells me.

But I know that he can't fall because they are very careful not to let the coffin swing too much.

"It can't fall," I tell him.

Two men take the places of the tired ones, and they make sure the coffin is secure; I hear my father's voice warning them to try to walk, to make certain not to drop the coffin. The rest of the men wipe the sweat off their faces; they spit often and walk toward us so that we can fall in behind them. We start out again. The noise begins anew, and now I feel different, but God is everywhere and He seeks the shade while we walk, while my grandfather bears the brunt of the sun. I feel thirsty. Yesterday my father and I came to the cemetery to see where Grandfather would be buried. It's at the first fork in the road, next to the wall. I spoke to Manuel and explained that my father had said that next to the wall was okay, that it wasn't necessary for him to be next to the sycamore. The sycamore is tall the way I like sycamores to be. As I raised my head to see it, I also saw the sky. The sky was blue; it seemed opaque in certain places, but clear, immense, as if it were sinking. It's like the sky today, intensely blue, bottomless, overflowing with heat and light.

Extreme Unction
6

By the power of this holy unction and His most pious mercy, may the Lord forgive you for all you have sinned with your steps, the sin that allowed you to intuit that your feet were created from within, from beneath your life, and for that reason they walked into the mine. May God also forgive you because you cried. May He forgive you for having lost your life, even though it was already spent, already useless. May He forgive you because at nightfall you felt steps you'd never heard before approaching. Was it your blood? Or was someone looking for you? Those steps could easily have been God's or those of repentance, but they were nothing more than those of your tired soul aimlessly wandering. After all, our souls tire when they spring forth within us, for these were born to be consecrated to God; but man is poor and stubborn and doesn't know how to accept that refuge, that road which never tires those who seek the Lord as it tires those who have not found Him. The road which never embitters as this one overwhelmed you, a road in which fatigue can never be found for it is the road of life, and only the forgiven will be allowed to walk it. Not in this village where the river is dry year after year until the rains make it come tumbling out of the hills, pausing at every bridge where all those men and women have crossed. The bridge that you used to see from the hills, from the orchard now turned green because your memories see everything green: the river, the hills, the grass, the trees, the pastures. Your feet reveled in the texture of the land, walking upon it as if the vegetation could reach within the mine and cover up the minerals. And the smell of grass, of rain, of dampness, of the river, all could reach you because that's how things were two years before your death. Later everything was just like your life had been; God's rain did not arrive and the sparse rain of your blood fled from you, taking your life with it. Then your steps ceased. They couldn't take you away from the suffocating sun, the daily heat, the unchanging sky and your lingering memories. May God forgive you for living. Had you repented of the life God gave you, He would have given you silence and repose sooner. But no, you managed to survive. You lived cursing everything around you, and in spite of everything you survived. You never withdrew from your favorite haunts, from your memories, but God looked upon you and heard you. Until one afternoon you foresaw His steps. In order to forget them you went outside, and one night you anticipated them in an incomprehensible dream. These harbingers you forgot, but one afternoon when you knew you would die the presentiment returned. You only thought you would die and were overcome by anxiety for the unknown, and when this anxiety vanished you thought that your premonition was those steps. You never discovered that God opened a door. It was as if an aroma or a light, an infinite door had been opened. You could always return, but you didn't know that. Because God will think about you, and once you are dead all hope is lost. The road that opened before you was a potent light and within it, as if against a door, your blood came to a halt never to flow again, for there was no longer any life from which to flee. You thought it was the darkness that blinded you forever, but it was His light that was near, closer than ever.

My Brother
5

When we were kids, Antonio and I used to walk along this creek. I don't remember if it goes all the way to the back of the mine. As a child after my grandfather's death I went up and down it many times. Occasionally Manuel would come with me, but I preferred to go by myself.

Everything is very quiet; cars pass near me out on the highway. The mountains seem dry, rugged. I go through the open gate. I see the graves near the entrance and a man smoking, seated on a bench in the shade of the office. I see the narrow path leading to the graves. It's very hot, but some freshness, some sensation of coolness seems to float in the air. You can sense something new as you come in. There's sun and quiet, and tombs, certainly, but one could stay here the whole day. I see the ruined tombs near the entrance, destroyed; some made of stone that are next to the wall are very old. There is a gigantic pine tree in front of another one with a small angel and a dome. The pine receives the sunshine and gives back only the shade. Farther down, a chapel can be seen with trees everywhere. I walk toward the office. The man greets me. I take off my hat and wipe the sweat from my head and face with my handkerchief. I feel my back wet with sweat. The cemetery is quiet, lonely. As a child I got used to coming here every day. I would come early in the morning, and I would sit underneath the sycamore near my grandfather's grave. I would spend hours listening to the sounds of the earth and the trees. I mention that it's hot, and the man laughs. He puffs on his cigarette and flicks away the ashes. I'm leaning against the wall with my hat beside me on the bench. Over there, down at the end, I see a man carrying two buckets of water on his shoulder. I see him only for a moment as he disappears among the trees. I feel as if the earth were cool.

"My brother died," I tell him. "I've already made arrangements for his burial, but I want to know the exact spot."

He takes a last puff on his cigarette and throws it near a grave with a fence around it. He adjusts his hat, says he'll look for the groundskeeper and for me to wait a little. He walks away from the office. I feel thirsty and hungry. I close my eyes and lean my head against the wall. I am sleepy and my head feels hot. I try to sleep a bit. The lonely sound of the cemetery surrounds me. My God, my God, a brother's actions are always painful, because otherwise what's the sense of having been born next to someone? It's as if I wanted to get away from here, but they wouldn't understand if I did. You would Antonio, but they wouldn't. But I don't really know why I came here. It's not because Pérez lives nearby, no, it's not that. At the other end of town, which I can't see from here because the hill where the mine is located obstructs it, you've remained behind, dying in peace without being bothered by me, so my presence would cause you no inconvenience. You need feel only the disembodied presence of your brother, his nearness, and not that of the man who has

distanced himself from you so that he can sit here falling
asleep on this bench. The image of the house comes to
my mind: the patio, the hill, and the river. I see María
dressed, walking toward me or sitting at a table, laughing,
putting her arm on my chair. I imagine that I'm caressing
her while she lies naked next to me. I see the streets; for
a moment I see a place in Talamantes, but it disappears. I
think I'm talking to Pérez; I explain everything and he lets
me go to work for him; we see that the truck is already
loaded and I must leave soon and make another trip to
Chihuahua or Durango. I try to open my eyes, and again
I'm aware of the cemetery, the noise of the birds, the silence, the tranquility of the place, of the trees. I open my
eyes very slowly and feel the sun of the hot day; it's almost
noon. I am very sleepy; my eyes are heavy. I remain quiet,
still, leaning my head against the wall, feeling the serenity
of the place, the silent, cool wall. I try not to think about
anything, but I keep thinking about María. Her smiling
face comes to my mind many times, or maybe just once,
but it lingers for a long time. I think about Antonio, about
his quiet acceptance of death, the slow way his life ebbed
away. He didn't protest because he was losing it. It was as
if he had used it so much, had worn it out so, that he
didn't want to hang onto it any longer.

I think about the funeral home, all the coffins, the
church. I need to see Pérez. I need that job. It depresses
me not to have found him. I hope Gregorio manages to
make that trip with the Vásquez brothers. I'll stop by again
to collect what they owe me. I hope I find them. I have
to move. Helena can't leave. Her brothers live too far
away, all the way down in Zacatecas, I think, or Queré-
taro. I don't know if they want to take her in, especially

with two children. As old and worn out as Antonio was, I can't figure out how he got together with Helena and had two kids. I want to keep my eyes closed, but I can't anymore. I need to eat something; I shouldn't have left without eating. I feel hot again, but it's really cool here in the shade. I hear the voices of men approaching. I open my eyes with difficulty. It's the man who was here before, and someone else is with him; they are angry with someone because of the waste of water. The other guy looks at me.

"Good afternoon," I answer his look without getting up. He's a man much like myself, not old. He sits close to me. He's wearing a hat soaked with sweat. His face is tense, unsmiling; he's still angry. He looks at me, waiting.

"My brother died," I tell him. "A few hours ago I was at the funeral parlor and arranged everything, but I want to know where he's going to be buried. I just want to look at the place."

He offers no condolences, nods in the affirmative, gets up, and before going into the office turns to the other man:

"This is the last time that I put up with that son of a bitch, excuse my language, sir, but next time everyone will have to take the blame. And you be sure to tell them, everyone will be blamed."

He goes into the office. Smiling, the other man glances at me.

"We've got a lot of problems here," he says. "It's the upkeep of the gravesites. There are very few of us, but we don't have much water . . . that's how he is."

He takes his pack of cigarettes from his shirt and holds it out to me. I take one; I'm thirsty and I ask him for some water.

"Yes," he says. "Here's a faucet."

He points toward the wall, behind where I'm sitting. There's a tin can on top of the faucet. I remove it and bend down to turn it on. The water is cold; I'm careful not to waste any because that's what they were arguing about. I wet my handkerchief. Now that I'm standing up, my body feels numb. I pass the wet handkerchief over my eyelids, and I feel relieved. I return to my seat. The man glances at me, his eyes half open as if he were looking at the horizon. When I put the cigarette to my lips, he offers me a box of matches.

"Here's a light," he tells me.

The man looks on as I light the cigarette. Then he turns and looks at something else as if he were deep in thought and weren't aware of anything around him. But he looks at me out of the corner of his eye as if waiting for some movement, alert. Suddenly he changes his posture without looking at me. I'm sleepy again. A typewriter can be heard in the office. You hear the keystrokes, very slow, separated one from another. I see the gigantic pine again. Its shade begins to cover the tomb. There is a small garden surrounding the grave; I can just make it out. On top of the tomb is a small angel covered by a white dome. I fix my eyes on it. I like the pine standing there tall as if defying the sun, very serene, saying something very masculine, very profound, in all this silence, my God. The other man comes out of the office.

"Come along, I'll go with you," he tells me. "I've got to go that way."

I get up and put on my hat before leaving the shade. I say goodby to the other man. I watch him raise his head a bit in order to answer me.

"Goodbye. Take care."

Again I feel the weight of the sun on my back. It's already noon. The man offers his condolences now, excusing himself for not having done so earlier. I see a man in the distance carrying water and walking with a boy toward the chapel. We stop and the man next to me shouts:

"I caught Manuel using too much water again. You better be careful because I won't allow it."

The boy keeps walking, but the other man stops. He's facing us.

"What does that have to do with me?" he answers. "Talk to him about it. I don't have anything to do with this."

"I'll tell you once again; you'll all be responsible for wasting water."

"We'll see . . . But okay, I heard you."

We keep on walking towards the rear. He tells me that the men understand only when he uses foul language, and for me to excuse his behavior, but he's got to do it this way. He doesn't say another word. We walk along in silence. The man walks beside me without wiping off the sweat, without using his handkerchief or his hand to wipe his forehead. I feel the sun burning me even more because of the water I poured over my head. I'm still hungry. I've got to get some sleep soon; tomorrow I'll see what can be done. I have to go back to see Pérez in a while. I need to know whether we'll get that job or not, and I also need to stop by and collect the money from the guys at the Ocampo mine; maybe they'll be there today. I should be well rested if I want to leave tomorrow with Gregorio. I couldn't go on a trip as I am. I couldn't. But the house is far away, on the other side of town. This walk is taking too long. Right there was where Grandfather Refugio's tomb used to be. I remember that year when all the storms caused the creek to rise and destroy half of the cemetery. It had rained a lot in the mountains, and the river and the brooks overflowed their banks; everything smelled like water, like slime. Antonio and I arrived just as the wall collapsed. I remember the pungent odor of dampness, the current as high as the tombs, inundating the walls of the chapel. There was a putrid smell, a stench of dead animals and roots. The ground was loose, at the point of being washed away. The graves of my parents were farther away from the creek and nothing happened to them, but Grandfather's had been covered with water since morning. I saw the sycamore, dark amidst the current. Two nights later, the current dragged away part of the cemetery, several of the graves. People said that parts of the graves were found as far away as Talamantes, but that everything else had turned into mud before it got that far. The roots of the sycamore seemed alive, some suspended in the air, others clutching the dark, humid ground.

"That part's new, what you see over there," the man tells me. "It just opened."

The sun is suffocatingly hot. We are almost at the rear edge of the cemetery. I see fewer graves. The earth is different; everything is walled, but the dirt is coarse, neglected. It's right on the hill. We walk for a while longer, and he points to a space marked out with lime.

"Here," he says. "Here it is."

It's at the edge of the cemetery. The earth is very dry and there are no trees; everything is still dry and covered with underbrush. This is hill country, I think once again.

Antonio and I used to come here when we were kids. But now the earth is dry, very hot, scorched. So much dry land. So much dead land. To rot here, here where I am among all this useless dry land, right on the side of a hill.

"Yes, it's okay," I say. "I only wanted to know where it was."

"The hole is dug a few hours before," he says. "Maybe we'll do it this afternoon, as soon as the funeral parlor lets us know."

The man wants to go back already. I turn around to look at the hills, at the sky. I can make out the highway and I feel the sound of the heat, the sound the earth makes in the heat, beneath the burning sun. That sun that has again burnt my head, it hurts me. I stamp on the ground with my boot. It's hard, hard and loose on top; the dust escapes even from the hand that's holding it. We start to walk back. It's only now that I feel that I've begun to kill Antonio within me. Now I know why death has to come to everyone, Brother. You start dying in each one of us, as if death could chase you everywhere, as if one death were not enough, but many deaths are needed many times over. And now I feel it. In the distance I see the trees in the other part of the cemetery. I'm thirsty. I'll buy a beer with the money that Gregorio loaned me, after I see Pérez. I don't know why I came, I don't know. I don't know what I feel inside, as if I were incomplete: it's something, something I can't comprehend. It burns like repentance, like hatred.

Offertory:
Lord Have Mercy

Our Father, save this Your servant because You have neglected him, even though he wanted it that way. And he fell prey to evil even though he asked You to help him, but he wanted it that way. Aid him from Your sanctuary because he found death on earth, he who never found enough bread when it was needed. From Zion protect him, oh Lord, even though You are unknown to him, because he didn't know what prosperity was, because he couldn't find an explanation; in the richness of the mine he could find only poverty, fear, dismissals, and the cave-ins that prematurely ended his misery. Be for him a fortress, for he never had a solid home. Give him Your salvation so that the son of iniquity cannot cause him further harm, because You left him at his mercy for a long time, because the Lord has already taken his life. Oh God of the living and the dead, be with him, cleanse him forever. Hear this prayer and may my request reach You. Be generous with him, Lord. Forgive him, Lord. Deliver him, Lord. You who hear us, by Your spirit save him from Your wrath. And save him Lord from the death that we must endure when we die. Save him from a tragic death, since he has already had a tragic life; save him from the punishment of hell and from all evil because he's already known and done many evil things. You who want everything good, even though we say that evil and punishment come from You, on Judgment Day let him live so that just for once he may see You and know You. Because the sickness of our lives came not from us, but was handed down from our fathers' times. We are born miners, lovingly nursed by poverty, and into the lap of hunger we bring our children. Give him, Lord, eternal peace, and may he perceive the light so that he may see, because we neither see nor breathe it in the tunnels. May his lifeless lungs accept and feel the light. Give him the light, Lord; his hardened lungs won't consume too much of it. We are blind, but wait for death in whatever form in order to receive Your forgiveness. Listen to us Lord, have mercy. Christ, have mercy. Lord, have mercy. Our Father, to him who never lived in peace, who never ate nor lived nor clothed himself in peace, Father, creator of all things, let him rest in peace. Father, let him rest in peace.

My Grandfather
7

We pass through the open gate which is lying in the dust.
The cemetery is quiet. Don Rodrigo approaches us with
a flower wreath and asks Manuel and me to carry it. I can
smell the flowers. The wooden frame holding the wreath
is hot and moist. The sun is already high and it'll be noon
anytime now. My father shows the way. I keep smelling
the flowers and I feel the heat of the wood in my hands.
I see three men leaning against the wall with their shovels
on the ground beside them. I tell Manuel to leave the
wreath resting against the sycamore, that it'll be all right
in the shade. I sit on the ground underneath the tree. Manuel is next to me. God has recognized this place; He seeks
the shade of the trees, and all the graves receive Him in
order to rest. Here it's different from the church. I take a
handful of dirt and open my hand to look at it. God is
breathing behind me, but He knows everything, including
what I am thinking. I get up in order to catch up with
Manuel. My father's forehead is wet with sweat. I look at
the black coffin; it is on the ground, maybe resting on
some stones because it looks tilted. My feet hurt; there are
rocks on the ground. Rocks used to annoy Grandfather
Refugio. I try not to think about Antonio, but I just remembered. The men pick up the coffin now. As they

lower it slowly into the grave, it swings against the sides. I don't scream, although I feel the breath building up inside of me as if God were also inside of me, next to my tears, but I don't scream. I wipe my eyes with the back of my hand so I can see better, but everything seems wet again, and I feel that I am hiding, or that God peeks out from behind the water in order to see, although He is slowly getting soaked. I hear the sound that the ropes make when they rub against the wood. Then my father throws a handful of dirt on top of the black coffin, and it appears as a blotch of mud, as if the coffin had just dirtied itself. I cry again, and this time I can't help but cry out loud, though I try to restrain myself. I also throw a handful of dirt onto the black coffin, and with the other hand I try to wipe away my tears. Once again I can feel the warmth of the earth in my hand as I squeeze it; I think about Antonio and I feel that we are different now, but that we are brothers, and I throw the dirt so that he may also throw dirt on my grandfather, and I listen to the sound it makes as it hits the coffin. Partly it is the sound of wood and partly the sound of the earth.

I see a bottle of mezcal. My father takes a big swallow first, and then he spits. They all start drinking and wiping their mouths with their hands. The men with the shovels throw dirt on the coffin. They bury their shovels in the soft ground near where I'm standing with my feet sunk to the ankles. Behind me, they want to make sure that everyone gets a drink and they ask who hasn't had a drink yet. All I hear now is the sound of the shovels as they sink into the ground and come out filled with the damp earth. As I walk, my feet sink deeper into the earth piled beside the grave. I make my way through the gathering and have to

walk on top of another tomb in order to reach the sycamore. I lean against its trunk. It's rough and dusty, but its
shade feels different. The sun is straight above our heads
now, almost ready to begin its descent on the other side.
It's past noon. My eyes are burning. I feel distant, I feel
very distant. But I don't want to be here, I don't want to
be here. I close my eyes and I don't want to hear the sound
of the earth, I don't want to feel the heat. Grandpa,
Grandpa, look at the ground that warms my feet. Grandpa,
Grandpa. I raise my eyes. There are several people seated
on the surrounding tombstones. At times my grandfather
would stop up in the hills and pick up a handful of earth;
he would hold it for a moment in the palm of his hand
just as I'm doing now, and then he would let it sift through
his fingers. At times he would walk all the way to the top,
and I could hear the sounds of the earth just as I do right
now, but even louder. It was the kind of sound that makes
you feel that the hills are alive, as if all of them could move
and pile up in the distance. Then Grandfather Refugio
would take off his hat and use his handkerchief to wipe
his hair and forehead, and he would spit once again and
then sit down because he couldn't breathe very well and
didn't want to get a nosebleed. And he would remain like
that, staring into the distance at the cottonwoods and walnut trees and looking up at the burning sun that fell like
a heavy hand on our heads. When it rains the earth is dark,
the color of the mesquite trees. I felt that the ground up
in the hills was like that, just like the earth I feel right now,
that I seem to hear right now waiting for the rain, dry, as
if it could only vomit bones. But he would tell Antonio
and me to throw our rocks higher up, away from him. He
would tell Manuel and me the same thing, but that was

later when Antonio no longer lived with us. In the morning, he would sit and watch us throwing rocks higher up the hill, so that later we could throw them further away, clear to the other side. When he walked through the hills, he would point them out: get that one, get those over there; throw them all the way to hell and gone, he would say. The rocks were hot, and when we picked them up we could feel their heat as if they were breathing. Grandfather Refugio used to say that dry things are bad, that it's the same with animals, that they dry up to the point of being useless. Up in the hills only the birds made a sound as they flew back and forth over the houses, chasing each other just like the ones I hear now over the voices of smokers standing around waiting for the men to finish throwing dirt into the grave. I wanted to kill one, but I didn't; I used to like to watch them play when I came back from the store. I'd just throw a rock that would fall to the ground far away from us and then sit down again. At dusk the hills stand sharply against the sky as if covered with ash, as if they were wet or it had rained, even though the murmur of the earth and the hills and the houses continues. I had to go near the hill and take a handful of earth to make sure that everything was just as dry as before. Manuel is walking toward me; he jumps over one of the tombstones to avoid having to go around.

"We are about ready to leave," he says. "They're already extending their condolences."

I see the people embracing my father. It's very hot. Manuel repeats that we should bring the flowers because they're just about finished. The men next to us get up to leave. I tell Manuel how I feel. He nods in agreement, but he doesn't really understand. He just asks if I'm all right.

Rodrigo picks up the wreath we brought. I remember what Antonio was like when I walked with him to the station. He exists only in my memory, but he's nearby, because it's as if his thoughts were my own. The earth is beginning to pile up, and they pound it down with their shovels. Then they place the flowers on top of the mound. Several people are starting to leave. I don't want to see. I don't want Manuel to talk to me. I don't want to see. I want my father to look at me, to touch me. I see the earth. I feel the same as when someone is looking at us and is getting ready to speak.

Rosary

The suffering, the joys, the mysteries, Holy Holy Holy, the holiest mystery forever and ever, amen. Hail Mary full of grace, Holy Mary forever repeated three times: Hail Mary, Hail Mary, Hail Mary and a fourth time Hail Mary for us. Save us God from all the saints and all the sinners and all the wicked and all the mine owners and all their mines, all their whistles, all the cave-ins, all the coins of the mines. We are already poor. That's enough. That's sufficient. We've learned our lesson. Our children are already this way and the children of our children, amen. Intercede with the fruit of your most pure womb, Holy Mother Mary, for we are your children whom you bore without sin, without pain. You were a virgin before giving birth, when you were still a daughter. You remained the purest virgin during birth and when you became a mother. After giving birth you remained a virgin when you were already a wife and for our sakes in the unbearable heat of our world where some can't breathe, don't have bread or food, and the little air we have leaves us slowly, ever so slowly. Holy Holy Holy All-giving All-knowing All-powerful. Forgiveness for the dead and for the living and for the unborn who nevertheless are doomed to be bitten by hope or by the earth that buries them. You, wife with the most beautiful body among women, look at our women and see what they are like: they get tired, they grow bitter, they stop being sweet forever.

Virgin Mary, Admirable Mother, hail hail hail, listen to us, help us, hear us, take us, find us, that our only riches be not abandonment. Amen to the infinite God, to the eternal Father, to the Son, to the Holy Spirit because in the sun which falls on this village we find the wages of our sins as it dries us and gives us nothing but hunger, only hunger. Lord Our Father, who is father of us all, glory to You, Lord, glory to You forever and ever. Hail Holy Mary full of grace, the Lord is with thee and blessed is the Son and blessed are His fruits. Holy Mary Mother of God pray for us sinners whose only refuge is the hour of our death, amen.

My Brother
6

There aren't many people on the street. I feel hungry. A little while ago the whistle at the mine sounded; it must be almost two o'clock. I'll get home late, but I need the money. I'll sleep the whole afternoon and get up at dawn. I have to make that trip with Gregorio. When I get back I'll go see Pérez. I'll insist; perhaps he'll need a driver for his semi.

"Good afternoon . . . I'm looking for Don Ricardo." The woman goes back inside. I need to know; I can't get by without money. Especially now with Helena and the kids.

"What is it?" says Don Ricardo, opening the door.

"I came to get my money, Don Ricardo . . . I've been waiting for a long time to get paid for the work I did in the last several months."

"We have many expenses right now with the mill. Nothing's working right," he answers. "I've already told you that, haven't I?"

"But I need the money, Don Ricardo."

"Yes, I know. But come back next week. We'll pay you everything then."

"No, I can't wait until next week. I need it today. You should've paid me two months ago. You always tell me the same thing."

"Come when I tell you, Refugio. I can't pay you today."

"No, Don Ricardo, you can get by, but I have many problems at home. My brother died and I need money. Pay me today. When you hired me, I did a good job, and Gregorio didn't mind waiting to get paid last, but I can't wait any longer; it's not right, not anymore."

"I'm telling you I don't have any money. Don't be so bullheaded; come back next week."

"I don't care, Don Ricardo. You're hiring others to make deliveries, and that's not right because you owe us, and you've already taken us for suckers and you need to understand we're not suckers. You're hiring others when you still owe us; I want to get paid today. I really need the money."

"You two didn't want to work; that's why we hired some other guys."

"You didn't want to pay us. I'm not asking for charity. I've already waited for a long time, and I've never let you down. I need the money today, Don Ricardo."

He looks at me without expression, but I stare right back at him, because he's really trying to screw us. He looks down and mumbles something that I don't understand.

"I'll give you three hundred pesos now. Next week we'll pay you the rest, understood? I'm giving you this money because of what happened to you, Refugio, and because I want you to see that we don't need to argue."

He takes some money out of his wallet and gives me the three bills. You are going to pay me everything and I mean every cent. Next week I'm not going to leave this place until you pay me. I've got a bad taste in my mouth, bitter. I take the bills and put them away and he tells me again to come back.

"Make sure it's next week, because it's not a joke that we need the money, Don Ricardo."

I'm not going to thank him, the son of a bitch. He looks me in the face, then turns his head a bit, getting ready to go back inside the house.

"Thanks anyway, Don Ricardo."

I hear him close the metal door and walk around inside the patio. At least I got some of my money. It'll get me through the week. When I finish the trip with Gregorio, I'll see Pérez. We also have to pay the priest next week. I'll come and stay in front of his house until they pay me. I bought metal from scavengers for Don Ricardo, and I took several shipments to his brothers' ranch, and I did everything else they asked me to; there's no reason for them not to pay me now, no reason at all.

All the streets are deserted. In the distance the only car in town approaches. The whistle at the mine sounds once again; it's two o'clock. I need to sleep. I won't be ready to go if I don't rest. Antonio's burial and the trip with Gregorio are too much for me. I have to get some sleep. I won't wake up until dawn. Let Julia take care of the wake. I'll get up for a while during the night, and then I'll go back to sleep. But it seems that nothing new has happened, that all this occurred a long time ago. It's not that I've forgotten Antonio. But it's as if I remembered him only part of the time. It's because I'm very sleepy, that's why. It's as if he were melting into a crowd of people and I was too tired to follow him. I didn't think about him before the way I have been these last few days. Not even when he came home sick accompanied by his wife, and he told me that he wanted to be with me. I said okay, that it was all right for him to come into the house. But it wasn't me who was speaking, but someone who spoke as if doubting or not understanding. I told María many things about him, everything that I remembered. Because you always love a brother; if not, what's the sense in being born together? However, María told me later that I wasn't talking about Antonio. And I understood, yes, I understood. Antonio became an old man in a few days, as if instead of being forty, he was over sixty. And it hurt me to see him like that; it felt as if someone were throwing handfuls of dirt in my face, and little by little I thought about other things while I was with him or when Julia's children brought mesquite pods to share with us and they would offer Antonio some. At times I even thought that it was my place to be there next to him, just to be there. At least we experienced the same things: the street filled with children, the hill, the houses, the walls of dry adobe, the laughter and the shouts of the children. At times the wind would bring us the noise of the mills at the mine, and I would be surprised to find myself sitting there next to Antonio, thinking about other things, but next to him, motionless, while the afternoon darkened, or watching the blood spurt from his nose and having him tell me that the bleeding was going to start again, and his wife, or at times my own wife, would clean his face, his clothes, and then he would close his eyes or he would keep them open for a while, opaque, as if lost in some thought that would make him close them again in order to think or to rest. Sometimes he'd say that it was too hot, that it'd be nice if it rained. In the beginning, during those first afternoons when he'd close his eyes, it would be in order not to cry.

But later he'd close them for no reason at all, just to rest a while. He didn't talk; I didn't know if he was thinking about something or if he was moving away from me as I was from him. He wanted it to rain, but around here you have to wait for years before it rains, and then the floods and then the drought once again, just like this year. And my wife would ask me about Antonio: why hadn't I mentioned him for so long? It's not easy to understand. Men draw apart, but brothers remain unchanged in silence, certain that each one has to be there, just because they're brothers. I stop for a minute. I see my sons; David looks at me. Julia's children come to greet me along with Antonio's youngest. I go into the corral. I hear my wife's voice down at the end. They have set the chairs outside the door. I smell the odor of the candles and the aroma of the food that Julia and my wife have prepared. There are only a few people, Julia's friends, seated next to her. I see the black coffin and the candles. I'm very tired; I want to eat something and get some sleep. First I'll clean up; I'll look for some water and wash up. Julia says that my brother-in-law will come in the afternoon and will keep watch over the body all night.

I tell her: "I'm tired, I want to get some sleep. In the morning I'm going out of town on a trip with Gregorio. I have to be rested."

She caresses me. I feel her warm hands on my face; she smiles at me. Outside in the corral I hear my wife talking.

"I'll get up for a while for the rosaries during the night, and then I'll go to bed again," I tell her. "We need the money I'll make from that trip."

I go out to the corral. My hair is messed up and I feel hot. The sun beats down on the dirt, on the peach tree.

My wife comes toward me. I'm aware of her scent. I give her the money.

"Here. We'll pay Rubén first because that's the most important debt." I turn on the faucet above the water trough. I bend over and feel the water. I close my eyes; I feel as if a rainstorm or an avalanche were descending. I lather my face and hair. I close my eyes and search for the water; I bend over again beneath the faucet and stay there, savoring the coolness of the water. I open my eyes and see the stone water trough. I keep throwing water on my face with the palms of my hands, which are now free of soap. My wife hands me the towel; I realize that she's standing next to me. At this instant I discover that I haven't been thinking about anything, that I was thinking only about the water, that I haven't been thinking about anything but the water. The very thought makes me feel more rested. I rub my face, my hair, my arms. But now I stop rubbing. I prefer to remain as I am, letting myself dry without a towel. I run a comb through my hair, which is still wet, and the water drips from my neck and my forehead. I go into our room. I feel the heat, the closeness, but no sun, at least no sun for once. My wife comes in behind me. I see the beds pushed up against each other; I let myself drop onto one and I lie on it raising my arms. I feel a bit sleepy, but not too much. I feel strange, as if I were incomplete, as if I were missing an arm. I'll try to sleep. I must eat something. I'll tell Gregorio that we'll leave right after the burial. We have to go collect our pay together, yes, together. I get up; my body is heavy. My wife is putting dinner on the table. Julia comes in now. I sit down and lean on the table, looking at the white dish, hearing my wife and Julia talking next to the kerosene stove. The soup is hot; I let it cool a little. I ask them to take some away, I don't want this much.

"There's no bread. The children ate it all a little while ago," Julia tells me.

I'm hungry. Yes, I feel sorrow. As if I were sad for something within myself, for myself, as if I were shaking, as if cold hands were roughing up the soul which I've carried inside for thirty years.

My Grandfather
8
(July 14, 1931)

It's early. The sun begins to warm the earth. The penetrating smell of the railroad station is everywhere. I am
sitting on a pile of rocks, waiting for Antonio. Everything
is lonely, empty. The railroad cars are motionless; they're
scattered across the field as if they were beasts grazing the
bare earth. From time to time groups of men pass through
the station, just like the ones crossing now by the water
pump. They disappear behind the cars. Now they reappear
carrying tools and shouting. In winter the station is very
windy; in the distance the dust rises and swirls everywhere,
from the water tanks, even through Santa Rosa, like a
multitude of trains coming into the station. I know all
about it because last winter I came here many times with
Antonio, and later, when I was by myself, I sat here to
watch. But today nothing stirs the dust. The sun beats
down throughout the station. I begin to feel the rumor of
the awakening earth in the oil of the railroad ties, as if the
smell were beginning to rise, to become a part of the air,
of the morning. The sun is beginning to warm the rocks.
From far off where the railroad tracks, the cars, and the
water tanks all disappear, the same heat which affects the
station has begun to accumulate along with the smell of
oil, wood, and steel. It's a smell that won't leave your body

for a long time. The station smells that way everywhere, even on the sides of the houses and along the creek that runs around the corner. I get up. Now I walk along these tracks; within each tie I find the smell of the train. I feel the oil mixed with dirt on my bare feet. People are beginning to gather on the platform. Antonio says that all railroad stations smell alike, as if they got their smell from so many trains making long layovers. Antonio has traveled since he was a kid. Ever since he was ten and he went to Escobedo and Jiménez.

The train is coming; down below you can hear it, you can make out its plume of smoke. I can't think; it's as if I were empty or with a lot of stillness inside, a stillness which I've never had before. Antonio can't imagine what I feel. I hear the whistle in the distance, very faint as when my sister Julia hides so we won't hear her crying. I feel that times have changed, not the heat but the days. It's as if they were different even though they began the same as always. I'll tell Antonio how I feel, ask him if he has ever felt the same way. He said he would get here the day before yesterday and he hasn't arrived yet. I know what he's thinking even though I can't see him, but I won't tell him anything. The people are all beginning to mill around on the platform. The whistle is louder now. It's noisy here next to the offices. All the voices blot each other out as if the people weren't here in the station where I've been pacing back and forth. I'm desperate, but in a quiet way. It's like when we need to ask for something and we're upset because we are losing our chance to do it. I'm tired; Manuel went to work at the store, but he stopped by to see me on the way. I told him I was tired, and he answered by laughing. I walked with him nearly to the store. The sun was burning hot if you left the shade. I told him that I would come by to pick up Antonio, that he'd arrive today, that I'd let him know if I could see him later. The train is climbing up the hill on the far side of the station. The whistle is loud now, full-throated, and sounds like a real whistle at last. And you feel that everything in the station wakes up because of the noise of the rails, of the whistle, of the cars, of the whole train coming to a stop before us. The wood siding of the cars is hot and dirty; I see the oil dripping down and mixing with the dirt between the rails. Everything turns into an odiferous cloud that hits me full in the face, the eyes. The people on the platform move around and there is a lot of noise and shouting, and the men on the train with papers beneath their arms gesture and shout at one another, calling out to the two workers who were waiting with tools in their hands. The train is still noisy, puffing steam; one can sense the life of the engine. The men in the office look out the door and see the people surrounding the train. The people are like me, but they are also like Antonio. Julia tells me that she'll be sad when he comes back. Dad doesn't say anything because he works here and Antonio in Veta Grande. But I'm the same. Antonio isn't on the train; he didn't come this time. I knew you wouldn't come today, and I came only out of a sense of duty, not to you, but to myself because even now I refuse to feel disappointed. I wanted to wait for you because it made me feel good. Besides, it's better that you don't come, even though you're my brother. There are fewer people now, and I'd rather leave right away and not hang around here any longer. There are people standing around in the street outside the station. As I walk along I can smell the blankets, the burlap sacks,

My Grandfather
9

A couple of men pass by carrying buckets of water. Their voices fade as they disappear down at the far end of the cemetery among the trees and the tombstones. The ground has a hot sound. I'm sitting beneath the sycamore. I removed the stones that were next to Grandfather Refugio's tomb; he didn't like them near him. Many times I saw him throwing away the stones himself. He enjoyed the trees and the river. The two blackbirds are on top of the wall turning their heads from side to side; it's a pair of grackles. I straighten myself and feel the sun, the hot blow of the sun. I walk toward the spot where the men disappeared. I find two stones. I pick them up. I feel their heat, but it's quickly gone. It's almost time to go back; I've been here for a long time. I feel a calmness similar to the one I felt this morning when I woke up. This afternoon I'll see Manuel. Yes, it's better for me to go to the store. Manuel doesn't understand, but he listens to me as if he did. He smiles and says yes, that he hadn't thought about that before. I hear the men again; they're behind me, walking toward the fork in the road. Their voices sound muffled as if in reality the trees and the tombs were also speaking, as if there were other voices present. I return to the sycamore and sit on the ground in its shade. The sky is very clear, very blue; it's past noon. I'm a bit sleepy, more because of the quiet than because I need to sleep. I've enjoyed this silence every morning that I've come to the graveyard. There's something new at home, a tranquility that I hadn't felt before. Ever since I sat and ate breakfast with my father. Mother served us coffee and beans while my sisters swept the floor. But all their voices and the noise that my father and I made sounded softer. I told my father that I was going to the station, that I wouldn't go to the store today because I was going to wait for Antonio. My father kept on eating, and after he finished, when he got up with his coffee in his hand, he told me not to worry too much, that I would understand later that Antonio was working.

There are the grackles again on top of the wall, moving their heads in all directions. I sit up smoothly and throw a stone; suddenly the black spots make a noise, frightened, and one of them flies toward the creek. Another falls next to the wall. I get up and once again I feel the sun above me, the hot hand of the sun. As I walk along I hear the heat; I walk around my grandfather's grave, looking at the wilted flowers that are receiving the sun's full impact. I bend over next to the wall and see the grackle bleeding from its beak. Its plumage is very dark, almost blue, and the blood is a soft mass on its face. Its eyes are closing. I feel pity deep inside me as I do when I remember many things that hurt. I pick it up and touch its warm, dirty, black plumage. Its head is drooping; it moves with the slightest pressure. I go around my grandfather's grave again and head for the sycamore. The grackle's eyes can no longer see and I know that it's dead. Still holding it, I sit on the ground in the shade. Its weight is formless. I close my eyes and feel as if I held sorrow in my hand, or a handful of warm flowers. I take some dirt and pour it over the bloody beak. The beak is open as if waiting to breathe any moment. I sit up again; I pick up the other stone and I throw it. I stop at my grandfather's grave and look at the flowers. They're worn out as if the sun had dried them up a long time ago. I feel the grackle in my hands, its legs hardening. Its feathers are almost blue, as if they were wet. I come close to the wall and I throw it over, all the way to the creek so that when it rains and there's a current in the creek it'll go all the way to Talamantes. I have to leave. Perhaps Manuel is still at the store. We'll stay there till nightfall so that I can tell him what's on my mind. We can go the station and go all the way to Villa Escobedo without saying anything, because we could get back by evening. I don't want Antonio to be the only one working. Here at the fork in the road I turn around to look at the sycamore and see Grandfather's grave as if he were lying down on that pile of dirt. From here the grave looks like a hill, like the hills that Villa Escobedo surely has, a hill full of houses and trees. "A handful of dirt is like a day," my grandfather always said. When we were tossing handfuls of dirt on his coffin, it was as if we were also throwing in his days, as if the days he lived, or failed to live, were piling up on top of him, and now everything was at peace.

The Blessing
of the Sepulchre

Oh Lord, You who in Your mercy grant peace to faithful souls, deign to bless this sepulchre and make its guardian an angel, a tree that won't mind keeping in its memory the sun that wears it out nor the mute voice that dreams of death in the depths of its roots. Leave it joined to the earth, anchored motionless for what seems an eternity just as we attach ourselves to a woman or to life, although life ends on the lips of death and its breathing abandons itself to sleep, even if in possessing a woman we may also sleep, even if while lying on her nakedness we close our eyes, not so much to explode inside of her with love, but to sleep. Oh, my Lord, to sleep as if a city or a flower were waiting for us behind the caresses. We reach down to receive the flower's aroma and its essence wounds us with a sweet voice that once forgotten we'll never be able to find again. And it's the tree that You have planted; it's an angel who sits next to the eternal sleep which ends our life with no wind to move it, without the murmur of leaves, without the sound of stars. But in the sepulchre, oh God, the tree is delivered unto the light; from its roots it rises into the night without fear or memories, and its fruits become afternoons, days, places because the world which surrounds it is the Presence which flourishes and lasts, which spreads out waiting for sleep.

Oh, merciful God who grants rest to faithful souls, deign to bless this storm, this deafening day that will uproot the night, *already subdued by the angry rains, making it one with the water bellowing in the creeks and in the river, fused once again as light and life are fused. And through Your mercy, let the creeks and storms tear down walls, earth, and sepulchres, let them rip out the side of the cemetery. And after the wound, when the lonely angel has nothing left to guard and sees its roots laid bare, let it also reveal its dreams and let old age and dryness explode inside it with a silence of days, of hopes. As it lingers on, let it age with the air and the afternoons and the evenings and the shadows of the nights. Let everything grow old as it tarries, because life can't wait and everything in You is exact, measured, correct, and nothing happens out of its time because during the wait we have perceived Your breath, but not Your voice. We have felt Your touch, but not Your presence. We have learned about You, God, but we haven't experienced Your life nor that of Your angels, and we depart from this life or this dream unawares, and no one knows who waits or what alone awaits us.*

My Brother
7

I sit on the bed surrounded by darkness. My eyes are still
burning; I rub them but the pain is worse. I'm thirsty; my
face and back are wet with perspiration. The room is air-
less. I turn on the light. Antonio's youngest son is asleep
next to my children. I search for a handkerchief. Standing
silently heaped are the table, the stools, the blankets, the
cots that were in the other room. I put my shirt on. The
mirror is already stained; it seems yellowish. I hope that
Gregorio comes so we can arrange tomorrow's trip. Or
perhaps he's already here. It's late already, eight o'clock
for sure. The money they paid me came in handy; at least
we'll have enough for this week; Lourdes and my sister
Marta will be able to stay for a few days more. I'll talk
with Pérez when I get back from my trip. But I'll also talk
with Rubén. It's not a bad idea to insist; it would be good
if I could find a job with Triplay. I'll turn off the light in
the room. I forgot my cigarettes; I don't see them anywhere. I probably left them on that bed where the children
are. No, they're not here. There I am, in front of myself.
I look at myself with suspicion, as if in reality I were like
that, like the mirror, yellowish and old. I look tired. My
tie is suffocating me and is crooked again. Soon I'll be
thirty, in three months. The guy looking at me from the
mirror is so distant that he can't hurt me. I feel guilty again.
I see I am full of remorse, as if I had really escaped and I

were the image in the mirror, old, motionless, dressed like myself for the wake. I rub my face with my hand and see the movement in the mirror. I turn off the light. I open the door facing the corral. I smell the cigarette smoke coming from the other room, along with the aroma of flowers. I see the lighted candles next to the black coffin. Lourdes and Julia are seated with some other women. My wife is next to Tabo's wife, down at the end. I say hello but stay here at the entrance. Julia offers me coffee.

"No, Julia, not now," I say to her. "Did Gregorio come?"

"He's outside. He came a while ago."

I go outside. I feel the night once again, but it's freer and warmer. I cross the corral. The street is dark. Next to the gate, close to the wall, the children are grouped together, talking. One of them is playing with Gregorio. I ask Augusto to go buy me some cigarettes. I walk a bit.

"Hi, Gregorio. No, keep on playing; we'll talk later."

I see the shadow of the street and the opaque lights strung among the adobe houses. The hill is near, on the other side where the street ends. I feel its enormous silhouette surrounded by darkness, like an animal casting its shadow upon us. I keep walking and listening to the children's voices. I stop; the children are playing close to the gate; I can barely make them out. Two or three of them are running nearby in the dirt and disappear in the shadow of the hill. Now they return, still running. I go back towards the gate. I enter the corral; Gregorio catches up with me. I go into the room. I see chairs along the wall beside the long, black coffin. The candles are lit; a wreath of flowers leans against the wall in the corner. The room is filled with the smell of flowers and candle wicks. I see my brother-in-law on the other side of the room talking softly with two neighbors. Gregorio sits next to me, quietly. His hat is on the floor next to the chair. My brother-in-law takes me by the shoulder. I hear the murmurs and smell candle smoke. It's very stuffy. The window is open, but with all the candles and the people you feel confined. Gregorio has become serious; I smile at him and pat him softly on the belly. I ask him for a cigarette. I feel the bitter smoke in my throat and it relaxes me, as if it were more than just smoke.

"I didn't find Pérez," I whisper. "He was at the lumber yard loading up a shipment to take to Chihuahua tonight . . . What's with the Vásquez's trip?"

"It's all taken care of. Tomorrow, early in the morning I'll load up. I'll wait until you bury Antonio, no matter how late it is."

Augusto is looking for me, but remains at the door. I signal to him and he enters with the cigarettes. He tells me that my wife wants to know if I want coffee. I don't want any and neither does Gregorio. I take a puff from my cigarette.

"I spoke with Don Ricardo," I tell him. "We should go together next week. They said that we don't want to work, that that's the reason they hired others, that it's our fault. If we don't go together and force them to pay us, they won't do it. Let the others know; we'll agree on a time and go together."

"I know that they already paid for the new trips," Gregorio says. "All those that they've contracted for during these last months. But, yes, it's better for all of us to go together and collect. I'll tell the others. I think that we could go next Tuesday."

"Gregorio, I already owe lots of money. Now with my

sister-in-law and her children it'll be difficult . . . As you know, when the company laid Antonio off they didn't want to pay compensation for his illness, only severance pay."

I open the pack of cigarettes and offer him one; he offers me a light. We light our cigarettes. I taste the smoke; I like it. We grow silent; Gregorio is thinking about something.

"I need you to give me a job on some of those trips," I tell him again. "Even on short trips until I find a better job. I'll see Rubén again to insist that I want a steady job with Triplay."

"It'll be difficult. No one wants to leave that place."

I've been aware of the black coffin; I've felt it next to me since I came in, with the same remorse and fear as when I was a child. A coffin is astonishing, the sheer weight of the thing. Looking at it is like a blow deep inside, like receiving an unexpected blow from a remote source insensitive to what's happening to us. I see the candles; a gray thread is rising from the flames. I'm still sleepy.

"I'm going now," Gregorio says. "I need to load up for tomorrow's trip."

I stand up with him. He says good-by to everyone with his deep, coarse voice and a wave of his hand. We go past the coffin. I smell the aroma of the candles. He takes leave of the women. He looks for my sister-in-law to offer his condolences again. I see a pot of coffee warming on the wood stove. We go out and pass among the men. The children are still by the gate, some standing up; others are seated with some objects which I can't make out. It's hot, but I feel better here. I walk with him for a little way down the street, and Gregorio talks about possible trips for the next two weeks. We get to the tree near Tabo's cantina; I say good-by to him and pat him jokingly on the stomach.

"I'll be waiting for you after the burial, no matter how late," he tells me.

I see him walking away, fat, enormous. I'm still here underneath the tree. I look at the hill, then towards the end of the street. I walk slowly, with no desire to return to the house. I feel tired. I don't deal well with these things; I'd rather leave. Two of Antonio's friends are coming. I see their work boots dirty, caked with mud. They offer me their condolences. We cross the corral. They greet the others standing outside. When they go in they hold out their hands to my sister-in-law and my sisters. Their trousers are old. One of them, without realizing it, is stepping on the stems of a bouquet of flowers. They stand still next to the coffin, without talking. They're as poor as my brother. All they can do is look and be near. Several times Antonio said that in the cave-ins when one is brought out alive, it's enough for the others to draw near, to be seen by the injured miner for him to feel better. Now they come forward to join with those who are near me. One of them is looking at me. Julia signals for me to come close. The rosary is about to begin. I'll tell Julia that I'll be next to the door. I go out and hear the voice of the old woman praying, sliding her fingers along the beads of the rosary. All the voices begin; the prayer is like a monotonous river which lulls you to sleep. Now I feel like drinking coffee. I hear the sounds of the night, of the heat. I feel that Antonio has forgotten me; or better, as if now Antonio had forgotten me once and for all, as if he had finally managed to do so. That's why I'd rather not think, though suddenly I feel that what one has lived doesn't matter, what matters is having lived; that it doesn't matter that he was a brother, but having been one, the experience of having been one. With our brother we live day by day; with a very close friend too, but the brother has the advantage of having started sooner, that's all. And the guilt feeling appears when things don't go well, when suddenly the brother or the sister lives somewhere else. They separate and there's more urgency then because we blame ourselves for the distancing, for the reasons behind the distancing. But I also wanted to know other things when we were together. I wanted to know if he also thought about Grandfather or Dad, not if he was thinking about dying, but about them. On occasion I would lower my eyes so that we wouldn't hurt each other. At times Antonio would be silent the whole afternoon, until it began to get dark. I thought that it would be easier for him to say it in the darkness, or for me to ask him. One time I told him about Bernabé falling off the mare and being confined to bed; he was happy and I even thought that he would talk. But he didn't say a word, and the smile remained on his face until it got completely dark. During the last few weeks when I brought him the mezcal, I was waiting for him to speak to me at some point. But he didn't do it. I felt Antonio was only my brother, and brothers perhaps understand one another. What I feel right now as I hear the rosary and the people is that it was all right not to talk, that it didn't matter to me. He didn't say anything. If he had said it at dusk without looking at me, with his eyes closed as if preparing to go to sleep, I would've told him not to think about that. Because no death is the same death even though you could die many times, even though we know we can die many times. Because I thought all this and not he, because I'm thinking about this and not him, it hurts me. Even though a brother wounds because he is like oneself, and precisely because he is like oneself.

That afternoon, night arrived walking slowly, as if it didn't want to arrive or as if night weren't going to come at all. It fell softly on the hill, on the town, on Grandfather Refugio, on his hands and breath. He heard it; he knew its smell, its hot taste. Grandfather Refugio sensed each instant as it became part of the night, as the afternoon became dark and looked down on the town from above, as it looked down from its seat in the hills and the stars, through the rafters of night at the men puffing on their cigarettes outside the houses, at the whole earth which wanted to set itself on fire hill after hill until it became a bonfire, at all the towns from El Real to El Valle and Villa Escobedo, to look at us searching for it in the darkness to pass its hands over what had been its earth.

He ate and held it in his thin arms to feel it against his belly, covering his cold legs, breaking it into pieces over the earth. He filled himself with night until he blackened, until he bled; little by little, until the night was no longer complete. Grandfather Refugio became night among the trees and the dry wood; he became night as thirst does, as the asphyxia of the mines dynamited his soul and hid it in a cave-in of days, of sentiments, of a metal that began to harden inside him until he carried a stone in his lungs with the asphyxia of many lives, of many moments abandoned in the earth, but not in free earth, but in its intimacy where all men are sown. He became night like an open shaft or an old gallery, and he seemed to sense within the smell of carbide a fruit of the earth, a voice that brought him seeds of nights to quench his thirst and calm his memories. An insatiable forgetfulness like the silence when one is alone. And the night began to sing amidst the cigarette smoke, from far off, from Escobedo, from off behind the days. It began to sing softly, very low, but then more loudly as if all the darkness were peopled by many, by many more.

My Grandfather
10
(July 15, 1931)

At this moment Antonio smiles at me, waving his hand. I
smile back at him. The serenity that I felt yesterday hasn't
changed. There are lots of people on the platforms, lots of
noise, creating a sound as though the train were still there:
all the boxcars, the engine, the wheels. A man from the
office crosses in front of me and blocks my path. I make
my way by pushing others and I see Antonio again, who
smiles as he speaks to me. He's just the same. It's as if the
noise, the shouts, had already happened. He extends his
hand and I shake it. He's still stronger than I and almost
causes me to wince as he squeezes my hand, but I don't
ask him to let go. He looks at me. I see the carbide lamp,
I can smell it. It used to be Grandfather's. We try to leave
by way of the offices. There are fewer people than yesterday. I feel calm, as on the other days when I came to
wait for him. Now he is here. I tell him about the store
and that everything is all right.

"Everything is going well, Antonio," I tell him. "Dad
thinks it's best for me to keep working at the store for a
while longer, maybe until the end of the year. I only need
to grow a little. Yes, I'll keep on working there."

I think about many things, but mainly I think that he's
my brother. I make an effort not to look at him, but I can

feel that he's with me, that we're here now, as if each one of us gained something by being next to the other. When I speak, I feel a well-being without changing outwardly.

"We buried Grandpa Refugio five days ago," I tell him.

I don't feel sad, though I don't tell him that I came every day to wait for him and he didn't come because he works in Villa Escobedo. I feel different. I feel that I'm Antonio's brother, but in a different way, as if I were the one who had just arrived and not him and we had noticed that my trip had changed me.

"The gravesite is fine. It's next to the first crossroad, close to a sycamore," I add.

We are now walking along the creekbed, next to the mine. I can smell the carbide lamp. I turn my head to look at it. We don't say anything about the road; we just walk along it without talking. But the calm I feel is in part owing to Antonio. It's as if Antonio complemented me or made me larger. He gives me a quince, saying that he brought it from Villa Escobedo. I want to tell him that I dreamed about Villa Escobedo, to ask him if it's like I dreamed it or if it's different. I ask him if there is a road from the station into town and if the trees seem sunken and bunched together and if one has to cross the same creek twice. He smiles, but he only looks at me.

"I dreamed about it. Manuel and I are planning to go there soon," I tell him. "We'll take the train, then we'll ride on a cart or we'll walk alongside the miners . . . that's why I was asking."

Antonio laughs and puts his hand on my shoulder without answering. I ask him again how to get there.

"To get there," Antonio says, "you need something else, not just crossing two creeks, but wanting to be there.

It's not the same as living here at home and working in the store, it's something else. Perhaps you don't understand what I mean . . ."

He stops talking and doesn't turn to look at me again.

"Then you cross the creek twice?" I ask.

"Yes, that's what Grandfather Refugio used to say, but you won't be able to recognize the creeks because it hasn't rained for a while and everything looks the same; besides, going there just for a day isn't worth it. If you wanted to work, even if you stayed with me, you couldn't. There isn't any work there. Only for very few . . . But you don't understand; you need to live a while longer. You have to be different over there because people don't understand. If you're not careful, they take you for a sucker and then you won't be able to do anything."

We walk along silently now. We are leaving the village.

"There aren't any more families of miners over there," Antonio says. "Or just a very few. They're only working in old shafts looking for metal scraps. They're scavengers. In Santa Bárbara they were beaten up by guards who stole their tools . . . But in Villa Escobedo the Gringos took everything. If you go, you won't find anyone in the streets. Everything is lonely, totally fucked up."

I throw a stone. I look for another one and I think of something; I throw it as if what I'm thinking were escaping from my hands, from me. I pick up more stones; I don't know whether they're the same ones or if they're different. This happens to me often these days. I hear him talk and these thoughts come to mind. It's better to let them go and walk along together, allowing the morning to pass because I have a lot to do at the store this afternoon. We can see the cemetery from here. We can also see the wall and above it the tops of the tombs and the crosses. The creek is dry, full of white stones. I feel a bit hungry and thirsty. Antonio is sweating and very tired too. He's my brother, of course he's my brother. I feel it because I understand what he feels; it's my duty. But I don't ask him because I feel fine walking along without talking, just being together, because it's as if we had taken care of all that needed taking care of, as if this were the way to take care of everything that happens. Dad says that you have to let time do its own work because it can do more than you can. We walk along like this, as if we had been silent for many days, every day that I waited for him at the station and he didn't show up. As if we had been silent, yes, because that's the way it had to be, because you don't need words. We are now in front of the iron gate. One feels a different heat, a different silence here. The cemetery is lonely. There is a sound in the earth, in the graves, a different sound, more intense, but different. In the distance a man is walking and disappears among the tombs. We walk more slowly, but still without speaking. I feel very calm, as I thought I would; all we need to do is to get there without talking because each one of my thoughts is mine alone. We are now at the first crossroad. I see the sycamore next to the wall; its shadow is huge and I can make out Grandpa's tomb. We needed to be here together, without talking. Because I, and no one else, needed this. Antonio sees the grave and approaches it. I stay behind. He's looking at it in silence. I feel the silence of the cemetery, the shadow of the sycamore, the trunk against which I'm leaning. I feel the sound of the tranquility which also emanates from me and joins with the calm of the place. The carbide lamp is on the ground, silent, next to the grave. Antonio walks toward the wall and looks at the sky; he's either impatient or tired. The sky is clear, blue. He takes his hat off now and I see his disheveled hair, his sweaty forehead. Antonio doesn't want me to work in the mine. And I'm old enough to work. No, not yet, but soon I will be. Dad said that Antonio doesn't want me to work in the mine. The birds fly through the sky from the creek and come to rest on the wall, further away from us. A man goes by with a water bucket and greets us; he's heading for the chapel all by himself. We start walking again on the hot ground. We don't speak. I feel freer, as if I had reached a beginning, not an end. Antonio looks at me now, not wanting to say anything, only looking at me. I feel that he's my brother, yes, but also as if he were someone like me, someone who is a part of me. I think about this as we walk out of the place. Everything is tranquil, quiet. We don't talk. Because in the silence there is something like us. And I feel different, as if the silence were coming out of my mouth, dripping from my lips, and I could hear it.

My Brother
8
(May 5, 1955)

The hearse enters the cemetery. I hear the footsteps of those who follow in its wake. There are only a few of us, but the footsteps echo loudly like a murmur of something that is being scattered, destroyed. I see the tombs. We are approaching the furthermost part of the cemetery. Here we are surrounded by stone markers, wooden crosses, or simply piles of dirt crowned with weeds and trash. I turn around: I see my nephews and one of my children with the miners, and in the distance the trees and the white sepulchres on the other side of the cemetery. It's still a long time before noon. A man walks rapidly in front of us. Everything is so lonely. I can't remember Antonio's voice; it seems that I've forgotten it as if it had walked away from me, and this was all I needed to make it irretrievable. Irretrievable for me in the same way that anguish disappears with the passing of the day. I can't accept that Antonio ever hurt me, because he was just like me. It's not just that I'm here and that I think I can remember this feeling, this moment. Rather it's the calm, the sensation of understanding something which I've forgotten, which I've already lived. There's no point in thinking about the same thing. I feel free simply by feeling that something happens, not that it happens this way or that, but that it happens. Because something is happening, I tell myself again, because I feel the change, the tranquility. We stop. At the end I see two men waiting for us next to an open grave. The men in the hearse open the back door to take the black coffin out. They lift it up and I go over to help them. One of the miners comes over beside me to help out. I'm aware of his smell; I see his black eyes, his stained teeth. I touch the coffin and feel the torn cloth covering it, sense Antonio's weight against the wood as we lift it. I am looking at the worn cloth, ragged where the nails hold it in place. On the way to the grave I feel an inner anguish, a pain which is beginning to stir. We place the coffin on the ground. I tell the men to go ahead. The miner who helped with the coffin is standing next to me. Antonio's oldest son is crying. Julia's children are holding the flowers. The men secure the black coffin with ropes and a strap and then lift it up. I see the coffin striking softly against the sides of the grave. It stops at the bottom, almost suddenly, as if not wanting to go any further. One of the men goes down to the coffin; standing on it, he places some bricks and mortar around the sides. I remember that they used to tell me when I was a kid that "A day is a handful of dirt." Each handful of dirt that you toss on top of the coffin eats away at the days; it's like piling up time till it catches up with you and lets everything rest in peace. The earth is lukewarm; it surprises me as I hold it in my hand. As I clench my fist, many thoughts rush into my mind and come to life; they seem to have a life of their own, for they haven't occurred to me before. "They wave their hands inside me," as I used to say as a child, "before coming to life." Before coming to this day, I mean. They want to take away my feelings, to take away what's been scattered around, because a curtain made up of many years has been destroying itself. Because a brother is this, a brother. He's like the hands that want to mold you, and you wait to see if these hands can really change you. And it's not worth it; it's not worth it to keep thinking about the same thing over and over. Not about Antonio, because he partially understood. I throw the handful of dirt on top of the coffin and it scatters all over the cover. It makes a hollow sound like a cracking eggshell or an old echo, waiting from the bottom of a long time ago to resound, to dissipate in my ears. I hear the handfuls of dirt and feel the movements of the miners who lean down to toss handfuls of earth in the pit. I bend down to hear the dull sound of the heat in the earth, the noise that the earth makes because of so much sun, so many weeds. I feel the heat rising from the arid earth next to my face, from this hill where they bury miners and other poor people, from this neglected land. I pick up another handful of earth and toss it into the grave. This time it's lost, you can't hear it. And I feel that the earth begins to fall on me like the aroma of many flowers or blankets, like an anxiety that can't defeat us.

I bury my family. I've always buried my family. Against a backdrop of debts, lacking the money to bury in peace those who have never experienced a good day, always filled with anguish and lacking enough bread for the women and children. My family, my family: always alone, yet always together. Neither my mother nor my father ever lived in peace, although I tried to help them. Neither did Antonio nor Lourdes's son. My sisters, damn it. Antonio, my brother, you and I alone on this earth all by ourselves.

I see the bottles of mezcal. One of the miners offers me

a drink. I taste the bitterness of the mezcal; it's as if my throat would spill out my voice, spill out the heat. I breathe anxiously because the mezcal is strong and because the death of a brother is as if a part of oneself also died. Even though I may feel the tranquility, even if I now look at the clear sky again, so blue, because time is like this: not something you change, but live. I see the land in the distance, behind the tears, behind all the coarse hills, the noise of the heat and the sun. I feel the firm ground beneath my feet, the earth of the surface, the earth where the sound of the heat produces another kind of sound: a sound not of more and more things, but of morning alone. It's time to leave with Gregorio. He must be outside, waiting for me. The earth piled up by the shovels is beginning to rise, to acquire the shape of a grave. Julia's children bring in the flowers. I look for the flower wreath to cover the grave. I feel the flowers in my hand. I look at them: they're oblivious to the heat, absurd in this arid earth. I get ready to leave. I must say goodbye here next to Antonio, say goodbye next to him and to all the miners who embrace me. But not to bid farewell to Antonio, because silence is good among brothers; it's good between us because you have to realize that it's not necessary to talk, that there is something very like us in the silence. Something that seems to live again, to be reborn, as if something inside us had reached its goal, but we don't know what it is in spite of its sucking our blood or kicking the shit out of us. Because things weren't made for us; they remain here or wait for a better time when all times are one. I see Antonio's grave and I feel the haste. For those of us who always live on the hill, it's the poor land of the dry hill, the hill for miners forever lost in the hills. For my grandfather, my father, my brother. Not for me. They knew it. I wasn't supposed to be a miner. There wouldn't have been a man left to bury the others. They needed someone who could outlive them, who could go on living through hell for a while longer. They meant to protect me. Protect me, so that I would shield them later, shield them from their debts, from the lack of work, driving trucks, searching for work as a truck driver, alone, with a different hunger. As if now Antonio were untouchable or unapproachable; as if this calm of the earth, this moment in which I don't feel like crying, in which I know the tranquility of the empty sky, the sound of this morning, of this calm, all of this, all this quiet in me, in this place—I had lived it all already. I had already known the silence and had already discovered myself because a dead brother is as if you had already disappeared or like you were already in danger, because he is like yourself. And you understand it. You understand.

Carlos Montemayor

Carlos Montemayor was born in Parral in the State of Chihuahua, Mexico, in 1947. His fiction has won the Xavier Villaurrutia Prize and First Prize for the Novel in *El Nacional*'s Fiftieth Anniversary Contest. A classical scholar and former teacher at the Metropolitan University in Mexico City, he also holds the distinction of translating the first complete edition of Sappho's fragments into Spanish.

About the Translators

Dale Carter and Alfonso González are Professors of Spanish at California State University, Los Angeles. Dr. Carter's translations include Julio Chiappini's *The Smile of the Asp and Other Stories* and *The Puzzled Alchemist and Other Stories*, as well as Usigli's *Crown of Shadows* and Sergio Magaña's *The Enemies*. He is the author of *Julio Cortázar: Life, Work, and Criticism*.

Dr. González teaches Spanish-American Literature, specializing in Mexico. He has authored *Indice de la Cultura en México (1962–1972)*, *Carlos Fuentes: Life, Work, and Criticism*, and *Euphoria and Crisis: Essays on the Contemporary Mexican Novel*.